The Last Straw

Margaret J. Baker

Illustrated by Doreen Roberts

Puffin Books

Puffin Books: a Division of
Penguin Books Ltd, Harmondsworth,
Middlesex, England
Penguin Books Inc., 7110 Ambassador Road,
Baltimore, Maryland 21207, U.S.A.
Penguin Books Australia Ltd, Ringwood,
Victoria, Australia
Penguin Books Canada Ltd,
41 Steelcase Road West, Markham, Ontario, Canada
Penguin Books (N.Z.) Ltd, 182–190 Wairau Road,
Auckland 10, New Zealand

First published by Methuen 1971
Published in Puffin Books 1974

Copyright © Margaret J. Baker, 1971
Illustrations copyright © Methuen & Co. Ltd, 1971

Made and printed in Great Britain by
Richard Clay (The Chaucer Press) Ltd
Bungay, Suffolk
Set in Monotype Ehrhardt

This book is sold subject to the condition that
it shall not, by way of trade or otherwise, be lent,
re-sold, hired out, or otherwise circulated without
the publisher's prior consent in any form of
binding or cover other than that in which it is
published and without a similar condition
including this condition being imposed on the
subsequent purchaser

Puffin Books
Editor: Kaye Webb

The Last Straw

'Where shall we go?' asked Bell, her eyes on the charred windows of the flat which had once been their home.

'Home with me, of course,' said Liza, who had been looking after them the night of the fire, and she squeezed all three of them, Guy, Rose and Bell, into her bedsitter. The next day she arranged for them to go and stay on her grandparents' farm in Somerset while their parents were recovering in hospital. Her grandmother would be glad of the extra money, said Liza, and besides that, she added mysteriously, 'So long as you seek there's a friend you may make, and then there will be no end to the things you'll find to do.'

But who was the friend? They soon found there were no other children on the farm, so it seemed quite a puzzle until, exploring in the attics, they found a dusty, cobwebby shape, an old corn doll made of stalks from the last sheaf of corn from the harvest. Musty as she was, Poppy the corn doll had character, and it didn't seem *too* surprising that she could talk . . . and call magic powers to transport them from wintry reality to share in those roasting summer days she had loved long ago. Somehow they all felt at home now, and ready to share in all the fun and misadventure their unusual companion landed them in.

This is another cheerful, likeable book by a popular author who has two other books in Puffins, *Castaway Christmas* and *Porterhouse Major*. It is an equally delightful and humorous combination of reality and fantasy.

For readers of eight and over.

Contents

Acknowledgements

For information about corn dolls I am indebted to:
A New Golden Dolly by M. Lambeth. The Cornucopia Press.
Corn Dollies and How To Make Them compiled by Lettice Sandford and Philla Davis. The Herefordshire Federation of Women's Institutes.
Somerset Folk-Lore by R. L. Tongue, edited by K. M. Briggs. The Folk-Lore Society.
British Calendar Customs by A. R. Wright. Published for The Folk-Lore Society by William Glaisher Ltd.
Introduction to English Folk-Lore by Violet Alford. G. Bell and Son.

For information about wheat I am indebted to:
Wheat by R. F. Peterson. Leonard Hill Books, London. Interscience Publishers Inc., New York.

M.J.B.

1 Fire alarm!

Being sent in mid-winter to stay alone at the farm in Somerset would have been strange enough, Rose thought, without anything else. Rose Tompkins with her brother Guy, and Bell, her younger sister, had landed at Knack Gold Farm like flotsam washed up on a beach after a storm. Everything that happened afterwards seemed part of the same emergency. The scorching heat of the flames which began it all seemed mixed with the heat of the sun that blazed down on the harvest fields at Knack Gold Farm.

Rose and Guy and Bell lived with their parents in a maisonette on the two upper floors of a tall Victorian house off the Cromwell Road in Kensington, London.

Rose had straight, fair hair which straggled to her shoulders. Her freckled nose was short and her mouth extra large. Guy always said smiling so much must have stretched it. Guy was dark and thin. Once Bell said he was like a horse-chestnut straight out of its shell. What most people noticed was his clear speaking voice and friendly manners. Guy never thought about either – they had just happened. Bell was the youngest. Arabella was her full name but Bell suited her best. Her short auburn hair swung straight on either side of her small face, and she was devoted to her dolls. Bell's dolls were a part of the family. The smallest doll was a clothes peg with a face chalked on the knob and a handkerchief cape. The largest doll, which had ringlets that could be curled round a drumstick, had belonged to her grandmother. In between there were doll's house dolls, a Dutch doll with no legs, and a rag doll, called Ethel, who had come from a boutique. The rag doll never fitted in with the others, but Bell did her best to make no difference, and she loved them all.

Everything about the Tompkins's lives had been ordinary till the night of the fire. The fire happened so fast there was no time to be frightened. Even Bell didn't think about the loss of her dolls – till afterwards, at least. On the night it was as if a great wave had hit them and sent them rolling in the surf. All that mattered was to keep alive, and yet, because the fire had happened in their own home, with a crumpled bag of bulls-eyes lying on the sofa beside a library book, and foreign stamps soaking in a saucer on Guy's mantelshelf, everything seemed peculiar and surprising as if what was happening must be happening to someone else. In snatches they might have been turning over the pages of a highly-coloured picture book. Even with the smoke smarting their eyes they had admired the fire engines, with their scarlet paint and chromium, which the firemen had taken so much trouble to polish. The trouble the firemen had taken seemed like a mark of politeness to them especially.

But without Liza Dawkings, the baby-sitter their parents had engaged to look after them that night, they would never have been able to manage, and what happened would have been far worse.

Liza Dawkings was plump and seventeen. She wore her hair long and her skirts very short. She worked in a London store in the daytime and did baby-sitting in the evenings to pay for extras. Most of the extras Liza wanted were clothes. She wore something new every time she came to look after the Tompkins. On the night of the fire it had been a white shirt with full sleeves, black stretch slacks, and black leather shoes with buckles.

'It's meant to look like a magpie,' Liza had explained. 'Folk at home call them thieving rascals, but their feathers are as bright and shiny as any you could find.'

Liza came from the country and she often planned her clothes to match the bright plumage of the wild birds. At home Liza had sung in the village church choir, clad in a blue cassock and a mortarboard hat, with white stretch socks and wooden-soled sandals. Liza didn't seem a lot older than Guy or Rose, yet Mrs Tompkins trusted her. She knew if Liza made a promise she would be sure to keep it.

'Of course, I'll take good care of Bell and the others till you're both back,' Liza had promised that Saturday night before their parents left for the theatre, and that was what she had done. It would never have occurred to Liza Dawkings to have done anything else.

Bell and Rose had been asleep in their room at the back of the house for several hours when Guy, whose bedroom faced the street on the floor below, heard a taxi-cab round the corner of the square and with a squeal of brakes pull up in the street below. Guy waited sleepily for the sound of his father's voice as he paid the driver and bade him 'Good night' before the doors of the cab were slammed shut and the taxi-cab sped on its way. Instead came a shout from his father, followed by the sound of racing footsteps, and sitting bolt upright in bed Guy began to cough because the room was full of smoke.

A minute later he faced Liza who was preparing hot drinks and sandwiches in the back kitchen.

'Father's taxi has stopped outside,' he said, 'but something's wrong. I heard Father shout out, then I smelt the smoke. It's half-way down the passage. It's coming in all round the edges of our front door, and the paint inside is burning off in bubbles. The whole main staircase must be on fire!'

Together they stood in the hall. Already along the foot of the front door flames crept like tongues of torn crêpe paper. From the main staircase beyond came the crackle of burning woodwork and a roar like the roar of a chimney when it is on fire. Above the roar came the sound of shouting, and for a second Guy thought he heard his mother call. Then there was a muffled cry and only the noise of the flames. Guy felt sick and beside him Liza was pale. He wondered if she had heard his parents calling also, but there was no time to make sure.

'We can't go out that way, that's for sure,' said Liza. 'We'll have to escape by the skylight in the roof. You go and wake the girls. I'll bring the step-ladder.'

The ladder was kept for house decorating, and the treads were spattered with emulsion paint. Smoke swirled round Liza's ankles as she tugged the steps out from the cupboard under the stairs. The hose of the vacuum cleaner twisted round her waist, and a bag of golf clubs crashed to the floor so that the balls rolled in all directions and skidded under her feet. But at last the ladder was free.

Guy helped her carry it up the last steps while Rose and Bell waited under the skylight on the top landing.

'We promised Mummy not to go on the roof any more unless she said so,' objected Bell. 'That was after the time we played at moon landings and an old lady opposite rang up to complain.'

'Just this once it won't matter,' said Liza as she mounted the step-ladder and pushed open the skylight. 'I'll give you and Rose a hand up while Guy holds the ladder.'

As first Bell and then Rose mounted the ladder and joined Liza on the roof, looking up through the open skylight Guy could see the chimney-pots outlined against the fiery sky. Below him at the foot of the stairs the fringe of the hall carpet was already ablaze, and the pages of the telephone directory that had been knocked off the table curled with flame. As he balanced on the top of the ladder and pulled himself up through the skylight, the ladder tilted below him and slid with a clatter down the stairs. But safe for the moment on the roof-top none of them cared. All that mattered was that they were together and able to fill their lungs with the cold air.

For a moment they paused huddled close against the chimney-stack. Through the billowing smoke in the street far below the fire engines looked like matchbox toys. Amongst the bright red engines aslant in the road-way stood the taxi-cab with its door flung open.

'That's the taxi Mother and Father came home in,'

said Guy. 'Directly they saw the fire they must have rushed straight across the road into the house.'

The moment he saw his sisters' faces white in the firelight he wished the words had died on his lips.

'Then where are they now?' asked Bell.

'And what's happened to them?' said Rose.

Liza's eyes met Guy's. He knew suddenly that she too had heard the cry which he had heard from the far side of their blazing front door.

'The sooner you're all safe and sound in the street down there the sooner we'll find out,' said Liza sharply. 'What we need to know now is how to get there.'

'There's a fire escape down the back of the flats next door,' Guy told her. 'Once, when we were on the roof before, Rose went down it to save a pigeon that was being stalked by a cat.'

Finding their way across the roof-tops lit only by the glow from the fire wasn't easy. Once, in the billowing smoke, Rose walked straight into the coil of a television aerial and she had to rip her dressing-gown free. Once, as they crossed the roof of the house next door, Guy's foot splintered the sooted glass of a skylight, and only Liza's steady hand stopped him from falling through.

'Couldn't we wait here and call for someone to help us climb down through the skylight like we climbed up through ours?' suggested Rose.

But with sparks still flying about their heads Liza decided that it would be safer to go on. It was also essential that they let someone know quickly that they were out of the building – and safe.

All the time they could hear the fire roar like an animal set free. With her hands held tight by Rose and

Liza, Bell thought the noise was like tigers roaming through a forest at night. All she wanted was to be safe in her parents' arms and sobbing as they held her tight. Now there was no time to cry. She had to keep up with the others and scramble as best she could through the maze of chimney-stacks. Her knees were grazed by the sooted bricks and her eyes smarted from the smoke, but nothing mattered except reaching the ground and racing to find her parents.

'It won't be long now,' said Rose. 'There's the fire escape just where we thought.'

Behind his sisters as they began the descent Guy wasn't so sure that he wanted their own escape to end and their search for their parents to begin. Now that they were so near to safety he was scared to think of what news they might be given.

'They'll be safe, don't ee fret,' Liza whispered as in the light from an uncurtained window she saw his face.

The cast-iron staircase led them down past the back doors of the neighbouring flats. They passed window-boxes still set with dead geraniums, cat-trays, bowls of hyacinths turned out after Christmas, and bottles set ready for the milkman. At last they stepped down into a yard and felt flagstones under their feet.

Looking up at the windows of their house next door they saw them filled with flames that blazed like shaggy chrysanthemums. In the flickering light they saw their kitchen's blue-tiled walls, and the girls' white-painted dressing table with the rag doll still smiling as she sat propped beside the looking-glass.

'Now we must go and find your parents and let them know you are safe,' said Liza.

The street in the front of their house was crowded with spectators. Hoses trailed across the pavement. From the top of two turntable ladders firemen directed showers of water into the heart of the fire – but nowhere was there any sign of their parents.

'You stay with Bell and Rose here,' Liza told Guy as they halted by the lamp-post that stood opposite their old home. 'I'll find out what's happened from the police.'

Waiting for Liza to come back seemed to take a long time. None of them even wanted to talk. The lamplight shone coldly down on their smudged faces. Bell had lost one bedroom slipper and blood trickled from her grazed knees. Rose's red candlewick dressing-gown, which she had been given for Christmas, was streaked with soot and ripped from the shoulder to the waist. Guy's face was set and the cord of his dressing-gown draggled unregarded in the mud. Mechanically Rose knotted it round his waist, but her fingers shook so much she was hardly able to finish the knot.

'If Mummy and Daddy aren't here looking for us where are they?' asked Bell.

'Liza will know,' said Rose. 'She's coming back now with that policeman.'

While they waited a crowd had gathered round them, but their faces were no more than a blur as Guy and his sisters listened to what Liza and the policeman had to tell them.

'Your parents are both safe,' said Liza, 'but they came back in that taxi after the fire had started and they were both hurt trying to break into the flat to find us. They've been taken to hospital now and they'll be told that you're all safe right away.'

Rose held Bell close because she was shivering under the blanket which the policeman had thrown round her shoulders. Beside them Guy asked the question that had to be asked.

'Are they badly hurt? Will they be all right?'

'Of course,' said the policeman. 'None of their injuries are serious, but all the same they'll need to be in hospital for quite a while.'

'Then where shall we go?' asked Bell with her eyes on the charred windows of the flat which had once been their home.

'Home with me, of course,' said Liza. 'I promised your mother and father I would look after the lot of you and so I shall.'

Liza Dawkings's bed-sitting room seemed as though it wasn't large enough to house an extra kitten, but somehow that night it sheltered them all. Rose and Bell shared the narrow divan, while Liza dozed in the basket chair, and Guy bedded down with the eiderdown on the hearth rug.

In the morning Liza shared out her own clothes. There was a jumper and skirt and her old school overcoat for Rose, a woollen mini dress which had shrunk for Bell, and jeans for Guy. None of Liza's shoes would fit Bell, so to make up for her lost slipper she wore two ankle socks.

While Rose and Bell finished dressing, Liza and Guy went out to telephone the hospital.

'Sister said your mother and father had a good night and are as comfortable as can be expected,' Liza reported twenty minutes later.

'And we can go to see them this morning,' said Guy.

'They both sent their love and told us not to worry. Soon they're sure they'll be as right as rain.'

After making the telephone call Liza had bought extra food for their breakfast and a Sunday newspaper.

'A lovely bit they've got about your Mum and Dad right on the front page,' she told Bell and Rose. ' "Heroic Bid at Rescue from Blazing Building", it says. Then there's all your names and how we finally got out the back way. On the way to the hospital we'll buy an extra copy and take it along for them to see.'

The newspaper story seemed unreal, yet as they ate their cornflakes and stared at the banner headlines it helped.

At the hospital Liza went to see their parents first while the children waited. For the first time since the fire, as they sat in the waiting-room there was a chance to think. Even on their way down the long corridors they had caught sight of the patients in the flower-filled wards lying in their red-blanketed beds. It had made them realize the gulf between the world in which people were well, and the hospital world where patients needed care before they could be well once more.

'However kind Liza is, one thing's certain: we can't stay in her room for another night,' said Rose. 'Her landlady would never allow it and there's not another bed-sitting room we could rent in her house. There's a card with "No Vacancies" printed on it put up over the front door.'

'And we shan't be able to live in our maisonette again for ages,' said Bell, 'even if we could cook and manage by ourselves.'

'Of course we shan't have to do that,' said Guy. 'Someone will look after us. There's no need to fuss.'

'Well, Liza won't be able to because of her job,' said Rose, 'and we haven't many relations. Only Grandmother in that hotel in Scotland and Daddy's brother in New Zealand, and Christmas-card second cousins – not even the sort who send presents.'

Their makeshift clothes made them feel as if they were playing at dressing up, and now that the dangers of the night were past they all felt tired and cross. They longed to see their parents, and yet now that the time was near they were scared at the thought of seeing them bandaged and in pain. Liza seemed gone for a long time. In hospital plays on television nurses always came to offer waiting relations cups of tea, but now only footsteps echoed in the bare passage outside. They stared at a battered pile of children's comics without seeing the words or the pictures.

Liza was smiling when she finally hurried into the waiting-room.

'Your father's in X-ray because they think he's broken his ankle,' she told them, 'but your Mum's ready to see you now just for a few minutes and everything's arranged. That's why I've been so long, but she'll tell you herself what's to happen to you all.'

Their mother lay in bed at the end of the ward. Her hair was still set as it had been for her visit to the theatre the night before. In spite of the bandages, when she saw them and smiled they forgot all their fears and ran into her arms.

'Liza has arranged everything,' she told them. 'You're to go to her grandparents' farm in Somerset.

Mrs Dawkings usually has paying guests only in the summer, but Liza has rung her up and she has agreed to take the lot of you in now. You'll be safe there till Daddy and I are both better.'

'It's Knack Gold Farm at Upper Barmington,' said Liza. 'You'll be there in winter – not the best time of the year – but things haven't been going too well with the farm lately and Gran will be glad to have the extra for your board and lodging. Apart from that there could be advantages specially for you. So long as you seek there's a friend you may make, and then there will be no end to the things you'll find to do.'

2   Knack Gold Farm

Knack Gold Farm was a long way from the road. It was set in misted fields on the top of a ridge of hills. Liza had put them on the train at Paddington. A Red Cross helper had met their train at Taunton and put them into a hired car which had left them at the foot of a stony track leading across pasture land to the farm.

'Of course we can manage from here,' Guy assured the driver. 'None of us has more than one suitcase and I'll help Bell with hers.'

The suitcases, like all their other possessions, were brand new. They wore new gum boots that shone in the rain, and new raincoats and sou'westers, which Liza had chosen in buttercup yellow P.V.C. for the girls and black for their brother. At their parents' request all their clothes and the cases had been bought from the store where Liza worked. Although the store was normally closed on Sundays, Liza had arranged for the children to be kitted out with all that they needed and for the goods to be put down on their father's account. The night-watchman had let them in on instructions from the manager whom Liza had telephoned.

Going with Liza from one silent department to the next had made them feel like a gang of criminals rifling

the store. Liza had enjoyed helping them to choose the clothes almost as much as they had themselves. None of them had had everything new before from vests and tights and stretch trousers to polo-necked sweaters, anoraks and nylon-backed gloves. Only Guy hadn't let Liza help him choose, except for the raincoat and one best floral neck-tie. He had bought a dark blue fisherman's sweater, grey flannels which would do for school and a duffle coat with horn toggles.

'You'll need everything warm,' Liza had told them. 'At this time of the year it can be mortal cold up-over.'

Making their way along the track to the farm they were glad they had taken her advice. A chill wind blew in their faces and it was raining. Mist clung to the fields. Now and then a cow loomed out of the driving rain and lifted her head to stare. On either side of the track they could hear the cattle tugging at the tough winter grass and breathing heavily. Once a wet muzzle brushed Rose's knee and Guy slapped the bullock on the rump so that it lumbered out of his sister's path.

'There's the house in that dip,' said Rose, pausing to mop her nose with the back of her new nylon fur fabric glove – for not even Liza had remembered to buy hand-kerchiefs. 'This path must lead to the front door.'

The farmhouse was built with stone which had been plastered and colour-washed pink. Here and there the plaster had broken away showing the stones beneath. The slate roof glistened in the rain. Old house martin nests clung to the eaves above the three rows of casement windows. A lawn and flower-beds flanked the cobbled path which led to the slate-flagged porch. A Welsh sheep dog, whose fur was heavy with baubles of mud, barked at them from the yard and fixed them with a wary eye. At the side of the yard water gushed from a fern-hung stone trough and flowed along a shallow culvert. Across the yard were the outbuildings, with great rounded stone pillars rubbed smooth by the cattle, and a brick stairway led to the hay-loft above.

'Everything needs repainting,' whispered Rose. 'You can tell they haven't much money.'

'Don't stare – let's get under that porch!' said Guy.

The broad steps in front of the porch were crowded with house plants. Rain washed over the leaves of a giant maidenhair fern set in a decorated china pot. Beside it a Christmas cactus still bore the last of its tasselled blooms, and a feathery fern twined between bamboo sticks.

'It's like Kew Gardens,' said Bell as Guy stepped between two geraniums and banged on the door.

A grey-haired woman in a white apron opened the door in answer to his knock. Her round face creased into a smile as she ushered them indoors.

'Dear me, the rain's fair bucketing down,' she said as they stood dripping in the flagstoned hall. 'It won't do to let they plants stand out in it a moment longer. Freshening up their leaves is one thing and a right old soak quite another. What the weather's coming to I'm sure I don't know. No doubt 'tis all they floating aeroplanes and folk travelling to the moon that turn it so troublesome.'

'Shall we help you to get them inside then?' suggested Guy.

'I'd take it kindly,' said Mrs Dawkings, with her face half-hidden by the leaves of the maiden-hair fern, 'only lift 'un gentle. That cactus has been in the family this past twenty years and you won't find a better this side of Barnstaple.'

Helping Mrs Dawkings to rescue the plants stopped them from feeling shy. None of them was anxious to talk about the fire, and to their relief Mrs Dawkings

25

behaved as if nothing out of the ordinary had happened to them. A wide, old-fashioned wedding ring shone on her well-scrubbed hand, and when she smiled her worn face lit up. Her voice was soft with a west country accent which Liza had almost lost. Afterwards none of them was able to copy how she spoke exactly. The sound only reminded them of the springing softness of a lamb's fleece, beech hedgerows afire with new leaves, and the scent of freshly-baked bread.

'Now I'd best take you straight up to your rooms,'

she said. 'After all your traipsing about you'll be needing your tea.'

She led them upstairs and showed Rose and Bell into a double room overlooking the front garden. There was a large brass bedstead and an electric stove was switched on before the black-leaded grate. Plastic roses were set in a vase shaped like a china boot on the chest-of-drawers beside a whitepainted swinging mirror, and lambswool rugs were spread on the worn, highly-polished brown linoleum.

'There's a stone hot water bottle in the bed,' Mrs Dawkings told them, 'and extra blankets in the wardrobe drawer.'

Guy's room was next door.

'There's a roach in a glass case and a stuffed sparrow-hawk,' he reported as they hurried down to tea, 'and pots and pots of plants. Geraniums mostly and those scented geraniums that straggle. One in the corner almost touches the ceiling.'

In the large, beamed kitchen Mrs Dawkings was already seated at the table with a man who they guessed must be Mr Dawkings. The table was set with a brown tea-pot covered with a knitted cosy, a fruit cake still in a tin marked 'Quality Street Toffees', a loaf of home-made bread, butter, and a honeycomb.

'These are the young folk Liza was on about when she telephoned this morning after you'd done swilling out the cow house,' Mrs Dawkings told her husband.

'Oh aye,' said Mr Dawkings.

He was a large man with fair sandy hair and a red freckled face. The brass stud showed in the collar band of his shirt, and he wore braces decorated with the faded heads of fox cubs. He cut them thick slices of bread without taking his eyes from the television screen which flickered in a corner of the room.

'Take a couple of pieces,' he advised. 'Likely you can do with a good bite.'

Eating the bread and honey they were glad that the farmer and his wife treated them with as little fuss as they would have treated an orphaned lamb brought in to be warmed back to life beside the kitchen stove.

The room was paved with bricks. A cream stove stood in the inglenook fireplace. Lodged in a rack above was a well-oiled rook rifle and a shepherd's crook. On the shelf below was a photograph of Liza, two china dogs, and a pair of brass candlesticks. Rose thought that it was as if after all that had happened they had been tumbled into a calm pool where everything moved slowly to the tick of the grandfather clock which stood in the shadowed corner.

Rose asked Mrs Dawkings about the name of the farm while she and the others helped with the washing-up.

' "Knack" is just some old word that means the last few blades of corn to be cut in a wheat field.' Mrs Dawkings told them as she squirted washing-up fluid over the blue-ringed china, 'though why it should be "Knack Gold Farm" has everybody foxed. We take the gold to mean the colour of the good corn that has always been harvested here, and so long as there's a fair average crop so that we can still make ends meet that's gold enough for us.'

'And will there be a crop good enough for that this year?' asked Rose.

Mrs Dawkings paused to wring out the mop. Her face was suddenly tired and troubled.

'In a hill farm 'tis hard to tell. After you've done all you can there's naught to do but watch the weather and hope for the best. This year since the winter wheat was sown we've had a sight too much rain, that's for sure; but anything can happen between now and harvest. Not much could tip it one way or the other. But over the past years we've had our share of bad luck and just one more setback, that most farmers would ride, could mean the end of us at Knack Gold Farm.'

Lying in bed that night Rose remembered her words. Even though she had known Liza's grandparents for so short a time already they seemed like old friends, and she hoped they would never be forced to leave the farm they loved so well.

Beside her Bell was almost asleep.

'When Liza told us about the farm she said there could be advantages to being here in the winter especially for us,' said Bell as she snuggled deeper under the blankets. 'What could she have meant?'

'Perhaps she thought there might be snow and a chance for us to toboggan,' suggested Rose.

'But there was something else that's puzzling,' said Bell. 'What did she mean when she said that so long as we searched there was a friend we might make, and afterwards there would be no end to the things we should find to do? I don't see who that could be because when I asked Mrs Dawkings if any other children lived near the farm she said "No".'

'Liza must have been thinking of someone,' said Rose, 'otherwise she would never have said it. We'll just have to wait till tomorrow. Then perhaps we'll find out.'

3 The corn doll

The next day the rain still fell. The mud came to the top of their gum boots when they ventured off the farm track and tried to open one of the field gates. Afterwards they watched from their bedroom window the sheep grazing in a field opposite. When one of the ewes shook herself the rain sprayed from her fleece like water from a sponge.

'We'd better go and look at the village,' suggested Guy after they had telephoned the hospital to inquire after their parents. 'It's still only ten o'clock and it will be ages before lunch.'

Donning their muddy gum boots and raincoats they made their way along the misted track past fields where the winter wheat barely sprouted in the waterlogged furrows.

'Mr Dawkings told me he'd never seen the wheat look so poor,' Guy told them. 'They've had nothing but rain since it was sown. No wonder they're worried.'

The village proved to be half a mile away. There was one shop which was also the Post Office. Aspirins and bottles of cough syrup were arranged in the window with tins of soup and bottles of gravy browning. Inside they bought picture postcards for their parents and Liza, paper handkerchiefs and peppermints with holes in the middle. Afterwards they looked at the church which was large and heated only on Sundays. They all signed the visitors' book and looked at everything mentioned in the printed guide. Finally they studied the names and inscriptions on the tombstones outside. When they straggled back to the farm it was still only half-past eleven, and the potatoes had only just been put on to boil for lunch.

Guy settled down to writing his postcards in the kitchen while Rose went in search of Bell. She found her in their bedroom with her nose pressed to the window-pane. A paper handkerchief was crumpled in her fist and she was sniffing.

'Lunch won't be much longer,' said Rose. 'It's stew with dumplings and treacle tart for pudding. Afterwards you'll feel better.'

'It's not being hungry that's the matter,' said Bell without turning round; 'it's knowing that everything was burnt – even that doll I didn't much like from the boutique. It's the things which weren't valuable that matter and no insurance money will bring them back. We've all got more clothes than we've ever had before, but there's not a single doll to play with, only that fish in the glass case and the dead bird.'

'Can't you make her a doll?' Guy suggested when Rose told him what had happened as they washed before lunch. 'Didn't Mother make her a golliwog once from an old pair of black tights?'

'We've only our new ones,' Rose pointed out, 'and your stretch socks.'

'Then we'll have to buy one,' said Guy. 'We've enough money with us and Daddy said to ask when we needed any more. Isn't there a toy shop?'

'Not nearer than Stonegate,' * said Rose. 'That's the next town and it's five miles away. Mrs Dawkings says the bus only goes once a week and their Land-Rover on market days. We'd be welcome to a lift but that's not till next Saturday, and Bell needs something to play with now.'

After lunch the winter afternoon seemed even longer than the morning. Guy departed to the barn where Mr Dawkings was mending a field gate. He and the farmer only spoke now and then as they worked. Mr Dawkings spoke of the gate as a female with a will of her own.

'She'll not hang easy if the hinges aren't just so. Take a bit of trouble now and it will save us a deal later on.'

Guy handed screws from a tobacco tin bearing a picture of helmeted soldiers embarking for the Boer War, and learnt how to countersink screws and to use a spokeshave.

In the kitchen Mrs Dawkings was busy making marmalade. After helping her wash the empty jam jars Rose and Bell wandered upstairs. There was nothing to read in their bedroom but old copies of the *Farmer's Weekly* stored on the top of the wardrobe.

Tiring of the pictures of prize rams and the problems of liver-fluke, Rose and Bell wandered into the passage. Already the light was fading but at the far end of the passage they noticed a flight of uncarpeted stairs.

'That must be the way up to the attics,' said Rose. 'It couldn't matter just to look. Mrs Dawkings said we might go anywhere except the pen where the bull's kept.'

* The market town of Stonegate bears no resemblance to the two other districts of that name – M. J. B.

33

Together they ran up the stairs and turned the key in the lock of the door at the top. The door swung open and they found themselves in the first of two attics which stretched along the length of the house. Rain washed the curtainless windows. There was the scent of old stored apples and damp plaster. Dusty newspapers lay on the floor and old tin and leather trunks stood against the walls.

Rose brushed the dust from the top of one of the trunks. The hinges creaked as she lifted the lid. In the corner lay a faded photograph in a cracked frame.

'That must be Mr Dawkings when he was in the army,' she said. 'Look, he's got a sergeant's stripes and he's really young.'

But Bell had wandered into the farther attic.

'There's not much in here,' said Rose as she joined her, 'only old meal sacks and that mangle.'

Bell took no notice. She was bending over what looked like a bundle of straw stuffed in the corner between the mangle and the wall and half-covered with plaster and cobwebs.

'For goodness' sake leave that alone. It will be full of spiders,' Rose warned as her sister tugged at the bundle. 'It can't be anything but rubbish.'

'It's not,' said Bell. 'It's a sort of doll.'

Holding the bundle on her lap Bell brushed away the dust and cobwebs, and they saw that it was a sheaf of corn which had been roughly fashioned into the shape of a doll. The stalks were bound with tarred twine. Ears of corn stuck out from the top of the doll's head and from the ends of the stiffly thrust-out arms. The eyes and mouth of the doll were made from tarnished brass

studs, which had once decorated a carthorse's headband. Two five-pointed stars formed the eyes and an upturned crescent formed a smiling mouth. A tattered skirt made of yellow cotton was fastened round the doll's waist, and a shawl made from a farm labourer's red-spotted handkerchief was pinned round her shoulders.

Cradling the doll in her arms Bell licked her finger and touched the straw. Under the dust it shone like gold.

Outside the window the clouds had lifted. A single shaft of sunlight lit up the corner of the attic so that the shadow of the straw doll with her outstretched arms danced on the rough plaster of the wattle wall.

'What ought we to call her?' Bell asked.

'As for that I'm not one for names,' said the doll in a high, dry voice that rustled like straw being pitched into a stable. 'Corn dolls aren't often saddled with them. No one's thought to pin one on me – not in all these years, and eighty or more that'll be come next Michaelmas.'

Dust blew from her ears of corn as she shook her head. Rose sat back on her heels and Bell sneezed.

'Then isn't a corn doll the same as an ordinary doll?' asked Bell.

'Not by a long shot,' said the corn doll. 'A race apart we've been right from the start, and when that was nobody knows. At harvest time when only the very last of the corn was left uncut one of the men would cut the last sheaf with his sickle and race with it back to the farm. 'A knack, a knack!' he would cry. 'I have un, I have un!' And all the girls at the farm would try to souse him with water before he was inside with the corn, for if none touched the knack the next year would be dry.'

'Then what happened afterwards?' asked Bell. 'Who was it made the corn into a doll?'

'The farmer's wife most likely,' said the corn doll, 'though some of us were made rough right out in the field with the sun beating down. Whichever way it was we were all decked out with flowers and yellow ribbons and set up in the big barn or the farm kitchen for the harvest supper, and there we were kept safe till the next year.'

'Why was that so important?' asked Rose.

The corn doll sat up very straight. The ears of wheat tumbled on her head looked for a second like a gold crown.

'Because of the power,' she said. 'The life of the harvest was in those last blades of wheat grown as they'd been by the spring rain and the heat of the sun. So long as the corn doll was kept next year's harvest was safe. However long and rough the winter, the growing time would come and there would be another crop of wheat. That's why the doll was kept till the next harvest was gathered, and then the new corn doll took her place.'

'Then how is it you're still here?' asked Bell. 'Wasn't there ever a new doll after you?'

'The old farmer died,' said the corn doll, 'upwards of eighty years ago, and the old ways went with him. I was the last doll fashioned in these parts. I've just carried on through thick and thin, though for a good while lately there's been none to remember or have need of me.'

No one spoke. The last rays of the evening sunlight had faded. In the dusk Bell rubbed the dust from the steel-studded brooch which fastened the doll's shawl.

'We need you now,' said Rose. 'There was a fire at home in our flat in London – that's why we're here. All Bell's dolls were burnt and now she hasn't one.'

'And we'll call you Poppy,' said Bell, 'after the poppies that grow in the cornfields.'

The straw doll rustled. In the dim light her eyes glinted and they thought she must be pleased.

'Poppy,' she repeated; 'it's plain but serviceable. Between friends it should do very well.'

And smiling she settled herself comfortably in the vacant place against Bell's shoulder.

4 Warming up

Afterwards as they washed the dust from their hands before tea even the bathroom seemed different. The old-fashioned bath with its lion-paw feet, the wash-hand basin with the viridian green stain under the brass taps, and the chipped cork mat all seemed unfamiliar and charged with magic.

'We can't not tell Guy,' said Bell as she soaped her hands with the amber soap she could see through, 'but what shall we do if he says it's all nonsense?'

'Whatever he says Poppy will show him it's true,' Rose told her. 'Poppy's not the kind of doll to be upset by anyone. After being in the attic all that time with rats, and bats, and snow drifting in under the tiles, nothing Guy might say would fuss her. Besides, on a farm she'll be used to boys. There would have been boys for bird-scaring, and plough-boys, as well as all the ordinary farm labourers.'

In the attic at dusk with the raindrops sliding down the cobwebbed window and the sheets of newspaper lifting on the bare boards, talking to the corn doll had seemed natural, but facing Guy, as he eased his Wellingtons from his stockinged feet in the back doorway, what had happened seemed different. The wind twisted the dark hair on the crown of his head like a tussock of grass.

In the darkened yard behind him doors banged and meal sacks, nailed to the lowest bar of the gates to discourage the lambs from wriggling underneath, tugged in the wind.

'You see she's not an ordinary doll at all,' Rose told him after she and Bell had done their best to explain about the corn doll. 'She's as different as a parrot is from a sparrow.'

'We didn't even notice she was talking at first,' said Bell. 'It just seemed natural like the noise the wind makes blowing across a field of corn.'

Guy only levered off his other boot and stepped in on to the brick floor of the scullery. Bell's face was pale in the light from the lamp fixed beside the back door, and her voice was clear.

'However impossible it seems,' she said, 'and whatever you say, we're sure she's magic.'

'And tomorrow directly after breakfast when it's light you can see that for yourself,' said Rose.

Guy didn't laugh.

'Of course I'd like to meet her,' he said, 'and I'm glad Bell's found a new doll even if she is such an extraordinary one.'

At tea, seeing Guy in his dark fisherman's sweater with doughnut sugar powdering his chin, Rose was glad he would be with them when they next visited the corn doll. It seemed as if Poppy must be the friend Liza had promised they might meet, and she wondered how much of the corn doll's secret their young baby-sitter could have known. The corn doll seemed friendly and yet part of a great deal that Rose didn't understand. Poppy gave Rose the same feeling as she had felt alone in the centre of a wood or when walking down a footpath at dusk.

At night the farm was more silent than any place they had known. All around them were the fields and the great twisted oak trees. Lying in bed listening to the wind in the chimney or the call of an owl Rose had longed for the sound of rumbling traffic, the patter of footsteps on the pavement, and the sight of an omnibus sailing past like a great red gondola in the night.

The next morning they woke to see their bedroom window feathered with frost. Petals of ice covered the cows' hoof-prints in the yard and icicles hung from the gutters. Directly after breakfast, clad in the hooded anoraks and slacks which Liza had helped them to choose, and with their brother beside them, they raced up the attic stairs.

'There she is in the corner near the window on top of the mangle,' whispered Rose.

The corn doll lay where they had left her with her head propped against the wall and her arms outspread. In the bright morning light her straw looked dustier than ever. A spider had spun a web between the ears of corn on the top of her head, and her red-spotted cape was marked by a bird's dropping.

'Do you mean those old rags wrapped round that bundle of straw?' whispered Guy.

'Hush or she'll hear!' warned Rose.

At the sound of their voices Poppy sat up with a jerk. Seeing Guy she twitched her cape straight and smiled at the girls.

'So you've come back,' she said. 'Now that the rain has cleared I thought you might have been taken up with something else. Company's strange to me these days, and small talk doesn't come easy.'

Her voice was husky and almost drowned by the sound of the wind rattling the slates above their heads.

'We think it's wonderful that you talk at all,' said Bell, using her thumbnail to rub the bird's dropping off the doll's cape, 'and we've brought Guy to hear so that he'll know all we've told him about you is really true.'

'I thought it was a game my sisters had just made up because they were bored,' admitted Guy. 'I'm glad it isn't. Bell needed a doll more than anything else, and we never guessed that she'd find one half as interesting as you.'

Poppy grinned towards him and tossed her head so that the corn rattled in the husks.

'We've asked Mrs Dawkings if we might play with you,' added Bell. 'She said we'd be welcome to have you to keep and she gave us some metal polish to rub up your brass.'

'And Guy's promised to make a pram so that Bell can wheel you out,' said Rose. 'There's a New Zealand apple box for the body and some real pram wheels we found on the rubbish tip.'

As Bell took out the tin of brass polish and a clothes brush the corn doll shook out her skirt, and a hibernating tortoiseshell butterfly tumbled from the folds together with a woodlouse.

'I must say that your company will be more than welcome,' she told them, 'and after so long I shall be grateful for a good brush-up – though at least in here I've kept more or less dry. Out in the barn I should have begun to sprout long ago. For a corn doll that's the beginning of the end. With the heads of corn on your hair and hands just anyhow, in no time at all you can be rooted to the spot.'

She paused as Bell polished her crescent mouth and then faced them with her eyes gleaming bright.

'Now for our outing – what's it to be? There's no need to wait for that pram, and none of you will want to dawdle about here – especially in this weather.'

Rose and the others stared.

'But where can we go?' asked Guy. 'It's freezing outside. Even the water trough is frozen solid. You need to run all the time just to keep warm, and Bell's chilblains are awful already.'

The doll sat up straight. Here eyes flashed and her freshly-brushed straw looked as stiff and strong as on the summer day when it had been cut in the cornfield.

'As for the weather I'll attend to that,' she said. 'No doubt I've the power still. Probably it's all the stronger nowadays for being stored up and not having been used.'

'Then you choose,' said Bell. 'We don't care what happens so long as we're warm.'

'Very sensible too,' said the corn doll. With her arms extended she shook her fingers so that a few grains of wheat tumbled from the heads of corn on to the top of the mangle.

Without needing to be told Guy and his sisters picked up the grains and held them in their fingers. In their cold hands the wheat felt warm. It's like the warmth of a freshly baked loaf, Rose thought, when you're carrying it home from the shop in a paper bag. The warmth from the wheat seemed to fill their whole bodies. Beside her Guy had unfastened the toggles of his duffle coat and

Bell's hand was on the ringed zip of her anorak. Rose realized that the whole attic was icy cold no longer, but warm.

Sun slanted through the window. The tortoiseshell butterfly which had tumbled from the corn doll's skirt had unfolded its ragged wings and was fluttering against the dusty glass. Without thinking Rose leant forward to unlatch the window. The butterfly paused for a second with its wings outspread on the sill; then it fluttered out into the sunny air and came to rest on the spiked purple bloom of a buddleia bush that grew in the yard below.

5 Powdered egg sandwiches

'Now if you're ready suppose we go down,' said the corn doll. 'One of you will need to carry me but I'm no great weight.'

Bell gathered the doll into her arms and felt her straw rustle as if a sudden gust of wind had swept through a field of corn. They knew as the doll sat erect with her head balanced against Bell's shoulder that she shared their own excitement.

'It's been a long time since I was out and about,' she told them as Bell adjusted her cape and spread out her skirt. 'There have been hijinks in the past, I can tell you, with one party or another. Young Kate and Tansy were game for anything, though I won't say any adventures I had with them bettered the time I had first with the little lass.'

The children stared. The sunlight glinted on the corn doll's eyes and her crescent mouth. When she laughed the sound was like grain being riddled in a sieve.

'You mean you've been out with children living like us at the farm before?' asked Guy.

'Bless you, yes,' said the corn doll, 'though it's not all children who have come to the farm that have taken up with me or I with them. Not by a long chalk. The need had to be there and the right feeling on both sides. There's children I've known who haven't given me a second glance as though I was no more than a wisp of hay to rub down their ponies.'

'Well, I think you're more exciting than any of the dolls I've ever had,' said Bell. 'Even the teen-age ones with wardrobes full of clothes.'

'Bell has always loved dolls,' said Rose. 'That's why she needed to find you so badly after all her own had been burnt in the fire.'

'That's what I meant about the need,' said the corn doll. 'For one reason or another all the others had it too. Till I'm needed nothing much can happen. I might just as well be a bundle of straw.'

'Do stop talking and come on,' called Guy from the top of the attic stairs. 'Downstairs the whole house smells different. Not of oil stoves, and split logs, and damp raincoats any more, but of apples which have just been picked and blackberry jelly boiling on the stove.'

No one was about as they crept down the stairs. On the landing the geraniums were gone from the window-sill and the window was hung with thick black curtains which looked faded and dusty in the sunlight.

'What ugly curtains especially for the summertime,' said Rose. 'Usually Mrs Dawkings likes really bright chintz.'

'The bathroom and all the bedrooms have black curtains too,' said Bell as she poked her head round the doors. 'Even Mrs Dawkings's room has them, and that picture you found of Mr Dawkings when he was in the army is on her bedside-table with a vase of sweet peas.'

'You shouldn't have looked,' said Rose.

As she spoke Guy called to them from the hall below.

'You'd better come down. There's something important that we'll have to decide.'

The hall was filled with sunlight that shone through the open front door. The hat-stand was hung with patched tweed coats, a faded umbrella, a hank of orange baler twine, a man's straw hat baked gold by the sun, a khaki haversack and a steel helmet. Nearby stood two buckets of water and a pump with a coiled length of hose. Guy was staring not at the steel helmet or the pump but at a bundle of tattered buff-coloured booklets which he held in his hand.

'What on earth have you got there?' asked Rose.

'They're ration books like they used in the last war,' said Guy quietly, 'and they were put out on the hat-stand with a shopping list ready for the grocer. Gran once showed me her ration books that she'd saved, and these are just the same with coupons inside for all sorts of food, even tea and sweets. But it's not just these ration books – Gran told me that at night not a chink of light was allowed to shine from her windows because of the enemy bombers who would have seen it during a raid. She had black curtains just like those we saw upstairs, and it was a stirrup pump like that one which she used for putting out some incendiary fire bombs when they were dropped on her roof.'

The girls stared. A spider had woven a web in the curl of hose piping and dried geranium petals floated on the surface of the buckets of water.

'You mean we've come back during the last war?' asked Rose.

'Right in the middle,' said Guy. 'It must have been

going on some time at least, because those blackout curtains were patched. And now what we've got to decide is if we ought to stay or to ask the corn doll to take us back.'

The corn doll rustled in Bell's arms and they hoped that she wasn't offended.

'Naturally it's up to you', she said with her eyes fixed on their anxious faces. 'We can go back in a twinkling, but this is one of the finest summers I can remember and with a climate like ours there's no point in being too particular.'

'Of course we must stay,' said Bell, and before the others could speak, with the corn doll clutched in her arms she raced through the front door into the sunlit front garden.

There was nothing to do but follow her. Out-of-doors with the sun hot on their shoulders there no longer seemed much cause to worry. Everything was peaceful enough. Bees hummed over the lavender and in a coop on the grass a Light Sussex hen clucked over a brood of chicks. It was as if the summer morning would go on for ever.

From Bell's arms the corn doll had eyes for everything: two young women in dungarees unloading bales of hay from a trailer in the yard, a litter of piglets with their mother in the sty, and the ten-acre field of sunbaked wheat.

'This is the gate Mr Dawkings and I mended yesterday,' said Guy as he swung it open for the others to pass through into the field, 'only now it's almost brand new. I remember Mr Dawkings saying it had lasted for the best part of thirty years.'

In the sunlight their eyes met. As the gate clanged shut behind them and Guy fastened the latch they knew that their decision to stay was sealed. Only the corn doll seemed unmoved. Her eyes gleamed as she inspected the wheat. Each blade and stalk reached straight towards the sun and the heads were heavy with the ripened grain.

'That's as fine a crop as any I've seen and just ready for cutting,' she declared as they walked in single file down the path close to the hawthorn hedge that bordered the field.

None of them thought of anything any more. It was

enough to be warm. The corn rustled beside them. Looking between the tall stems was like looking into a golden forest. A lark sang above in the cloudless sky. Scarlet pimpernel and heart's-ease bordered the path and a blue butterfly rested on a dusty stone. The warm air filled their lungs and the sun burned their faces.

'We'll have to take off our tights and winter vests,' Rose decided. 'Wearing them under our winter slacks we'll bake.'

Guy waited with the corn doll in the shade of a hawthorn while his sisters undressed on the other side of the hedge.

'That's just what Kate and I had to do the first time,' said someone with a giggle as they rejoined Guy with the clothes they had discarded bundled in their arms. 'Only with us it was worse. Clothes hadn't been rationed then, but to save those we had Mother had made us skirts from a policeman's cape and our car rug. We had sea-boot stockings besides made from oiled wool, and Kate was wearing a sort of hood called a Balaclava helmet. She'd knitted it for the troops only she couldn't send it because it turned out miles too small.'

Looking up they saw two girls grinning at them over the top of a blackberry bush. Their cotton dresses were faded and had been lengthened with material of another colour. Their legs were bare and their toes wriggled through the torn toe-caps of their tennis shoes. The taller girl had freckles and red hair, and the girl who had addressed them wore a sun hat with a hole in the crown and a tattered brim.

'Upon my soul – it's young Tansy and Kate!' said Poppy, sitting erect in Guy's arms. 'Of all summers to

49

have chanced on this is a fine one and no mistake! As if all those winters we've spent together weren't enough. From Rogation Sunday in May till Michaelmas I've always had as time off for my own affairs. Now I have to come up with you in full summer and it will mean coping with the pack of you all at once.'

'There's no need to be huffy – it's just bad luck,' said Tansy. 'Kate and I have left you in peace all this summer. Directly we heard the first cuckoo we put you in your usual place in the attic well wedged in by the mangle and we weren't going to disturb you till Mrs Dawkings lit the first log fire.'

'But that's where we found her yesterday,' said Rose, staring at the two girls. 'Only with us it's winter and freezing cold as well as being ages later. We're staying at the farm because our flat in London was burnt out and we've nowhere else to live.'

'But we come from London too,' said Kate. 'Our house is in Edwardes Square at the end of Kensington High Street.'

'We were sent to the farm at the beginning of the war as evacuees,' said Tansy. 'That's just a beastly official sort of word for the children who had to leave their homes in the towns and be taken in by families in the country where they would be safe from the bombing. Mrs Dawkings took us and she couldn't have been kinder, but with her husband in the army and only two Land Girls and a boy to help on the farm, she's always busy and having the corn doll in the wintertime has made all the difference.'

'We found her the day after we arrived,' added Kate. 'When we were at the reception centre waiting to be billeted they gave us two tins of corned beef and two pound bars of chocolate for emergency rations. Tansy ate all her chocolate the first night we were here. The day after she felt dreadfully sick but directly we found the doll even she felt better.'

'You'll find she gets you into dreadful muddles,' said Tansy. 'Twice we've been so scared we've stopped letting her take us anywhere, but we've always started again. All her trips are to places where it's summer, and the farm is so freezing in the winter we can't bear not to go. Once, when even our face flannels had frozen, she took us to a desert island and Kate had such dreadful sunburn after that Mrs Dawkings had to send for the doctor.'

'But so long as we're really warm we don't care what happens,' said Kate.

'That's what we thought too,' said Bell. 'Only we never guessed we should turn up right in the middle of the last war. When Guy found out he was so worried he nearly made us all go back.'

'Not just because we were scared,' said Rose, 'but because it wouldn't be fair to our parents while they're in hospital if anything was to happen to us here.'

Guy flushed but Kate and Tansy didn't laugh. When she spoke Kate's eyes were set on a ladybird crawling up a blade of grass by her foot.

'Anyone would be a bit scared but there's no need to worry because of the war. The air raids are terrible in the big towns. We know because Mother's an Air Raid Warden in London and Father's a doctor at one of the big hospitals, but nothing ever happens here. All we ever hear is the enemy bombers going over on their way to drop their bombs somewhere else.'

'But though the war has gone on and on so that you think it will never stop, we've never even seen an incendiary bomb or had a chance to use that stirrup pump in the hall,' said Tansy.

'And we've never been half so frightened as we were once when Tansy and I wished ourselves back into the middle of a really awful battle between the Saxons and the Danes right here on the farm,' said Kate. 'The Danes mostly had hair the same colour as mine and when the Saxons discovered us hiding in the corn I was nearly beheaded as a spy.'

'Of course I whisked the pair of them home pretty sharp,' said the corn doll. 'No harm was done though the crops were fired and the harvest that year must have been in a poor way.'

'And now will you come to pick blackberries with us?' said Kate. 'Mrs Dawkings gets extra sugar for jamming and bottling so we'll need quite a lot, and any that are over we'll sell in aid of the Red Cross.'

Guy looked at his sisters. The corn doll rustled as Bell took her in her arms.

'Of course we will,' said Rose as she took an old punnet basket from Tansy's hand.

By lunch time they had cleared the best of the blackberries from several fields and wandered some distance from the farm. At last, with their baskets full and juice staining their pricked fingers, they sank down by a haystack and Kate unwrapped a packet of sandwiches.

'They're only margarine with beetroot and powdered egg,' she said as she offered the sandwiches round. 'Our two ounces of butter ration for the week is always used up by Monday. And the powdered egg tastes like musty indiarubber but it fills you up.'

'We never thought of bringing anything to eat,' said Guy as he and his sisters hesitated. 'If everything's rationed won't it make you go short?'

'Of course there's heaps,' insisted Kate. 'Usually we have real eggs off the farm but the new pullets aren't laying yet.'

'And we've bread pudding besides,' said Tansy, 'as well as a whole blazer pocket full of Beauty of Bath apples.'

'At least I did bring a slab of chocolate from the shop,' said Rose.

'And I've a banana I meant to eat at eleven,' added Bell. 'It's a bit squashed but inside it should be all right.'

Kate and Tansy stared at the bar of chocolate and the banana.

'That chocolate would be both our sweet rations for a week,' said Tansy, 'and we haven't seen a banana for more than a year.'

After their meal they were lying half-asleep in the hay when far in the distance a siren wailed, with the notes rising and falling across the silent fields.

Beside them Tansy and Kate never looked up. Kate was nibbling the core of an apple and Tansy had her tattered straw hat tipped over her eyes.

'Wasn't that an air raid warning?' asked Guy. 'And shouldn't we take shelter?' From the distance came the sound of aircraft, and now and then they felt a thud as if a giant fist had struck the ground.

'Of course it was a warning,' said Kate as the trails of

the fighter planes chalked the cloudless sky, 'but there's no need to take cover out here. It's different in towns. There the Air Raid Wardens make you stay under cover till the 'All Clear'. Sometimes in Stonegate we've been stuck in a shelter by the cattle market for hours.'

'Those puffs like cotton wool are made by the gunfire from the fighter planes,' said Tansy, raising the straw hat from her nose to stare at the distant battle, 'and that silver ball with the sun shining on it is the parachute of one of the pilots who has baled out.'

'If you'd really rather, we could find a ditch or take cover in that wood over there,' said Kate as she tossed away her apple core and glanced up at their faces. 'Just at first you might feel more comfortable.'

'Of course they would,' said the corn doll. 'You might at least try to be more thoughtful.'

But the plane with black crosses on its wings was over their heads before they could move. They heard the cough and splutter of its engine and saw flames streaming from its tail. Barely the height of the haystack divided them. As they stood staring, too frightened to move, their eyes met the eyes of the pilot in the cockpit. They saw his helmet and goggles and the barrels of the guns which protruded from the plane's wings, yet as they stood helpless outlined against the haystack, the pilot never fired.

'It's a Messerschmitt 109,' whispered Kate as they stared after the crippled plane. 'The pilot will never clear those trees. It's bound to crash!'

A second later the earth shook under their feet. Trees splintered in the wood and a column of oily smoke rose into the air. Afterwards there was silence.

They stared at one another, white-faced in the sunlight. Bell clutched the corn doll in her arms and Tansy shook as she reached for her sister's hand.

'Come on,' said Guy. 'We'll have to go and see. There's no one else near enough to help.'

They ran together over the rough grass. Bell stumbled as she tried to keep up with the others. The corn doll jolted in her arms with the sun glinting on her eyes and the heads of corn shaking on her head.

'Tansy and Bell ought to stay behind,' said Guy as they reached the outskirts of the wood and smelt the burning plane.

Tansy halted but for a moment Bell defied him – her eyes bright with tears.

'Someone ought to look after the corn doll,' whispered Rose. 'Just one spark could set fire to her straw.'

Leaving the two younger children the others plunged on through the trees. The fighter aircraft was smashed against the stump of a splintered oak like a model aeroplane Guy had once made to fly in Kensington Gardens. The flames which they had seen coming from the tail had spread towards the cockpit where the pilot sat slumped over the controls.

'There may be ammunition left,' warned Kate. 'The whole plane could explode at any moment.'

'But we've got to get the pilot out,' said Guy. 'We can't do anything else.'

'Come on then,' said Kate. 'Let's try!'

The pilot roused as they struggled with his harness. Close to, with his goggles pushed up on to his forehead, he looked only a few years older than Guy. His eyes were weary and red-rimmed. At first he barely saw them, then he blinked and signalled to them to go away.

'Not come near! *Danger!* Leave me! Go back.'

The words from his cracked lips were like sentences from a half-forgotten school textbook.

'Of course we shan't,' said Rose. 'Undo your harness – then give us your arms quickly.'

The flames were hot on their faces as together they lifted and tugged. The pilot was too stunned and exhausted to do more than move feebly, but at last as they struggled to free him a length of canvas and metal broke from the side of the cockpit. Sparks showered in their faces but with a final heave the pilot was on the ground beside them. Together they stumbled away from the blazing plane, and Tansy and Bell raced forward to meet them.

None of them paused till they reached the haystack. There they sank down on the tumbled hay beside the baskets full of blackberries which lay where they had left them. Guy helped the pilot unbuckle his helmet. His hair was cropped short and darkened with sweat. Above his pale forehead it shone ginger in the sun. With one of their paper handkerchiefs Rose wiped the oil and smuts from his face. Afterwards he lay back against the hay with his eyes closed. A fly landed on his cheek. As it reached his nose he brushed it away and stared up at them.

Guy and his sisters knelt in the hay beside him with the corn doll cradled in Bell's arms, while Kate and Tansy had risen to face him. Still white-faced they stood close together, with their heads held high and the sun bright on their faded dresses and ragged shoes. He's their enemy, Rose thought, and remembering all that Kate and Tansy had told them about the war she felt sick because she was afraid of what they might do or say. Near by a grasshopper ticked in the grass and the silence seemed to last for a long time.

'If you're thirsty,' said Tansy, 'perhaps you'd like some of our blackberries. We've picked plenty.'

As the pilot grinned and reached forward to take a handful of berries, they heard the sound of a police whistle from the direction of the farm. Peering into the sun they saw a policeman making his way towards them across the fields.

'You'll have to go now,' Kate told Guy and his sisters. 'You mustn't be here when the policeman arrives.'

'But what will happen to him?' whispered Bell with her eyes on the pilot.

'The policeman will hand him over as a prisoner-of-war,' said Kate. 'He'll be all right. The prisoner-of-war camp is quite near here and it's not at all awful. Mrs Dawkings's sister goes there sometimes with a mobile canteen for the guards.'

'All you need to do is hold the corn in your hands and wish!' whispered Tansy. 'Just like you did when you came.'

'But my grain's lost,' said Bell as she searched in her pockets. 'It must have fallen out with that banana.'

'Then take another from my head and be sharp about it,' said the corn doll. 'There's no time to dawdle here.'

With the wheat grains clutched in the warm palms of their hands, and while Bell held tight to the corn doll, they wished.

For a second they saw the German pilot blink in astonishment; then the sunlight faded. The fields with the solid figure of the policeman walking towards the waiting group beside the haystack disappeared. They were standing by the mangle in the attic once again. On the window-ledge a robin perched with its feathers puffed out against the cold, and the newspapers at their feet shifted in the breeze that blew up from the bare boards.

6 'All is safely gathered in'

It took some time to make the pram for the corn doll. Guy set the apple box on wheels and fixed a handle. Afterwards Rose and Bell upholstered the box with a pale blue plastic foam bath mat which they bought from the hardware van that called each month at the farm. The van sold everything from weed-killer to artificial flowers, chromium-topped jam dishes, ladies' rubber girdles, hedging gloves, and shepherds' crooks.

'Now we ought to give the pram a coat of paint,' said Guy when he had finished sandpapering the wood. 'Mr Dawkings says so long as we clean the paint brushes properly we can use up any paint left in the tins in the wood-shed.'

They chose for the box powder blue paint left over from painting a farm trailer, and yellow left over from the bathroom for the wheels. When they had finished there was still some of the yellow paint left, and with it Rose painted a border of ears of corn all round the carriage. It meant waiting for the blue paint to dry underneath, but somehow after their first adventure none of them was in a hurry. Making the pram gave them time to think.

'Magic's all right so long as you know the rules,' Rose said as she finished the last ear of corn. 'The trouble is

Poppy seems to make them up as she goes along, or else she expects us to know them without being told.'

'But what happens doesn't seem like magic to her,' said Bell; 'it's perfectly natural like us switching on the television or someone going to the moon.'

Even when the pram was finished there were still extras.

'We'll knit her a coverlet from odd balls of wool,' said Rose. 'Mrs Dawkings has given me a lot from her knitting-bag; and we'll make a rainproof cover from one of those black polythene boiler-fuel bags. You know how Poppy feels about getting wet.'

'That's as fine a baby carriage as any I've seen,' said Poppy when they finally carried the pram upstairs to the attic. 'A harvest waggon bringing in the last load all done up with flowers and with me on top couldn't have looked better.'

She sat in the pram on the patchwork quilt with her skirt spread out and her head held high.

'Now all we need is an outing,' she said, 'and a fine summer day.'

Outside snow lay piled in the yard. The steps leading to the hay-loft were no more than a pillowed drift. Downstairs in the farmhouse sacks lay in the passages to soak up the footprints of half-melted snow. The farmer was busy from dawn to dusk carting hay to his stock, and the cows stood all day in the yard on a trodden carpet of straw.

'Wouldn't you rather be just wheeled round the farmhouse indoors?' suggested Rose. 'Won't taking us somewhere else be too tiring for you so soon after the last time?'

'Gracious no!' insisted the corn doll. 'With Tansy and Kate I was on the go from morning till night. In the Christmas holidays it never stopped.'

'Then do let's go,' said Bell. 'Being warm even for a little while would help my chilblains.'

Rose met her brother's eye. She knew he was reluctant to say what was in both their thoughts.

'We enjoyed our last adventure and we liked Tansy and Kate a lot,' she said, 'but this time could what happens be a bit less exciting? The war was ordinary to them but it wasn't to us. Tansy and Kate had had time to get used to it slowly, but for us it was like jumping in at the deep end of a swimming pool.'

'When you can't swim very well,' added Guy, 'and

we did feel mean about sharing their rations whatever they may have said.'

'Besides that bread pudding and the powdered egg made Bell feel sick,' said Rose. 'Mrs Dawkings had to send Guy to the shop for digestive powder specially.'

The corn doll rustled her straw and they hoped she wasn't offended.

'Your little sister is quite better now, I hope?' she asked anxiously. 'There were no lasting ill-effects?'

'None at all,' said Bell, 'and it might easily have been something else I ate, not that pudding or the powdered egg at all.'

'Then I will do my best to make this trip less hair-raising,' said the corn doll, 'but mostly it's hit or miss. With magic you have to take the rough with the smooth – tummy upsets included. Now what's it to be – shall we go or would you rather stay at home?'

'Of course we'd like to go,' said Guy.

'But let's put on sensible clothes first,' insisted Rose. 'Guy's always all right in his shirt and jeans but it was feeling so hot last time that made Bell and I both feel queer.'

Five minutes later Rose and Bell rejoined their brother and the corn doll in the attic clad in their tomato-red brushed-nylon nightdresses and slippers. Liza had helped them to choose the nightdresses which had long sleeves and ruffles edged with lace.

'Hitched up they'll be quite cool,' said Rose, 'and they were all we could find.'

'Mrs Dawkings said we'd catch our death of cold,' added Bell, 'when she saw us running upstairs and Rose told her we were just dressing up.'

The three of them shivered as Poppy shook the grains of wheat on to the patchwork pram coverlet.

'Now pick them up and wish!' commanded the corn doll.

The warmth began deep in the marrow of their bones. It was like the first glow from an oil lamp or the comfort of a bath towel which has been aired on a heated towel rail.

'The attic has changed,' said Rose, looking about her; 'now it's a bedroom. There's an iron bedstead with a tin trunk, and a washstand, and a deal chest-of-drawers, and hooks fixed to a board in that alcove.'

Blinking in the sunlight they saw that the walls were papered with rose-patterned paper and that white cotton curtains edged with pompoms hung at the window. The floor was covered with a square of linoleum patterned to resemble a carpet.

'Now I've done it,' said the corn doll, shifting excitedly in the pram; 'this is the little lass's bedroom. Sarah Tinkley was maidservant at the farm when Victoria was queen. The larks Sarah and I had together you wouldn't credit. No more than ten years old she was when she came to be trained by the mistress. She was smart at her books or she wouldn't have been let off school so young even then, but for all her learning she wasn't past playing with dolls. Not that she'd ever had many to miss. One there had been made from the sole of an old shoe with the heel for a face, and another fashioned from a sock so full of holes that the stuffing fell through.'

As the corn doll fell silent, they heard the sound of organ music from the distance. Peering from the window they saw small flags circling above the distant trees.

'It must be a roundabout,' said Rose, 'and those shadows moving up and down must be made by the swing-boats.'

'Then it will be the Revels and Sunday School Outing in the park of the big house,' said the corn doll. 'Once a year, just before the Harvest Festival, everyone's invited by the Squire and his lady.'

As she spoke footsteps sounded on the attic stairs. A moment later a small, thin girl of about twelve stood in the doorway with her eyes fixed upon them.

An apron begrimed with coal dust was tied over a print dress which reached to her ankles, and on her feet was a pair of rough leather boots. Her cap was awry on her dark curls and her face was smudged with soot and tears.

'Why, 'tis my own old corn dolly riding in a grand chariot and with company!' she said, racing across the room to hug the doll. 'And I thought you were put safe away for the summer.'

'And so I was till these young folk rummaged me out,' said the corn doll. 'But what's amiss?'

'It's that dratted kitchen stove,' Sarah Tinkley told her with a sob. 'Since six this morning I've been at it, puffing with the bellows and putting on candle ends, but still it went out and the mistress's cakes were spoiled. 'You're not to leave for the Sunday School Treat till it's re-lit,' the mistress said before she sailed off, and I've been since dinner getting it alight. Now the afternoon's half over and I'm still not changed.'

'A tartar she is and no mistake,' said Poppy, 'but if you make haste you'll still be in time for the Tea. If you're agreeable we'll all go along with you and you can show Bell here and her brother and sister the way round. Their home in London was burnt down in a fire and they've been at Knack Gold ever since during the worst of the winter weather.'

'We came back to the past with the corn doll just to keep warm,' added Guy.

Sarah sat down on the bed and giggled as she looked at his sisters.

'And fine frights you look,' she said. 'Clothes to suit were something the corn doll never did fuss over.'

'These are our nightdresses,' explained Rose. 'We knew it would be hot and all the clothes we packed were winter ones. At any rate they're long enough, though we never guessed it would be such ages ago.'

'Close on eighty years,' said Poppy with pride. 'We've travelled back from the future. Queen Victoria's great-great-grandchild is on the throne of England and you'd scarcely recognize the farm with a machine for milking in the cow parlour, and a cream and chromium stove in the kitchen that needs no blackleading at all.'

'Never!' said Sarah. 'Would you credit it!'

Her spirits rose all the time. She and Poppy were clearly old friends.

'But for Sarah I'd have been put into the dust cart or on to a bonfire,' Poppy explained. 'When the old farmer died and the new young master brought home the mistress I was on the kitchen mantelshelf poked up in a corner behind the tea caddy with pipe spills and turkey feathers and a good deal of dust. A right spring clean the new mistress was set on. Not a speck of dust would she let lie or a cobweb swinging from the rafters. "And that old heathen thing is to go first of all, Noah

Dawkings!" she told the master. "Such rubbish and idle imaginings! Your father may have harboured her but I'll have no truck with her. Nothing but a heathen idol she is, with that vain silly grin, and out she shall go along with any other superstitious nonsense." Then she took me to the door and tossed me out. I landed in the midden along with a horseshoe from the barn door, and a holed hag-stone that had always hung in the stables as a charm to keep off witches and to quieten the cart-horses.'

'And that's where I came upon her the day I was hired,' said Sarah. 'Half-buried in muck and none too sweet-smelling, but finding a doll for company was just what I needed and I soon had her freshened up, with all her brass shining and a new neckchief for her shoulders.'

'All through the winter she kept me hidden up here in her own trunk,' said Poppy, 'while from Rogation Sunday till Michaelmas I was free to rest or go about my own business.'

'We've had such adventures those cold winter nights from candleshine till midnight as you'd not believe,' said Sarah. 'Anywhere warm we've been, with lions and tigers in the jungle, to Australia with the kangaroos, and up the Amazon with a missionary. A gold rush we've seen, and ancient Egypt with the Israelites forced to make bricks without straw, and the corn doll going in danger of losing her limbs, and Brighton beach with whelk stalls and pink sticks of rock and all the waves shining like the best salmon's scales on a fishmonger's block.'

Afterwards they waited in the outer attic while Sarah washed and changed into her best dress.

'She'll not be long,' Poppy assured them as they stared uneasily at the hooped frame of a crinoline hanging on the wall, beside great leather trunks and hat boxes made stout enough to travel on the outside of a stage coach. 'Sarah's only the one dress so there'll be no chopping and changing.'

Five minutes later Sarah stood before them in a sage green dress which reached almost to her ankles. It was fastened at the neck with a band of velvet. Small buttons stretched from the neck to the hem and double strips of braid decorated the dress, reaching from her narrow shoulders to the knee. With the dress Sarah wore white cotton gloves and stockings, a flat straw hat decorated with cherries and her old thick boots. Her cheeks shone from washing and her eyes were bright.

'It's a lovely dress,' said Rose. 'You look just right.'

The grounds of the big house were crowded as Sarah escorted them through the wrought-iron gates and up the wide avenue which led towards the house.

'It's like a Victorian picture come to life,' whispered Guy.

Under the trees a little girl with blowing golden hair galloped across the park on a piebald pony. Children crowded round a donkey taking their turn for rides. Tall, loop-framed bicycles were propped against the park railings. Tub traps, dog carts, landaus, and a wagonette stood in the broad drive before the house, and babies in great frilled bonnets sat in high-wheeled prams. From near by came the thump of wooden balls at the coconut shy, mixed with the notes of the steam organ on the roundabout, and the delighted cries from the passengers in the swingboats as they rose and fell in the sunlit air.

'The foot races will be over now,' Sarah explained, 'but there will be pony jumping and tea for Miss Swithin's Sunday School Scholars in the big tent.'

It was very hot. They drank lemonade, made from bright yellow crystals, out of thick clouded tumblers. The corn doll sat in the pram surrounded by bunches of cornflowers, pinks, and tight-budded roses which Bell had bought from a little girl with a basket full of penny nosegays.

'You ought to have been more careful,' Rose told her after she had made the purchase. 'That little girl might easily have noticed that your pennies had Queen Elizabeth's head on them instead of Queen Victoria's. If only you had waited Guy would have given you some old pennies from his coin collection. He stuffed some of them into his dressing-gown pocket when we escaped from the fire.'

The curate swooped down upon them just as they were entering the tea tent. He was tall and dressed all in black except for his high starched collar. Bending towards them under the leafy trees he reminded them of a gentle-faced giraffe.

'Why, it's Sarah Tinkley from Knack Gold Farm,' he said with a smile that showed his long ivory-coloured teeth, 'and with several young friends whom I don't think I have met.'

'If you please, sir, they're visiting,' said Sarah.

'From London,' added Guy.

'But if the tea is only for the Sunday School we can easily wait outside,' said Rose. 'Only Sarah thought it would be all right.'

'Of course,' said the curate with his eye on Guy's

open-necked shirt and jeans and his sisters' improvised dresses, 'any friends of Sarah are friends of ours, but what's this that you have in the baby carriage?' he added as they turned away. 'Why, I do declare it's an old-fashioned corn doll and as fine a specimen as any I've seen.'

He bent to inspect the doll more closely, and she returned his stare with unblinking eyes.

'She was at the farm, sir, when I first came,' Sarah told him. 'The mistress took against her and turned her out as of no account and I've had her ever since.'

'No account indeed!' said the curate. 'That corn doll is as handsome a bygone as you could hope to find. If you're agreeable, I'd like to have the loan of her for the harvest festival decorations in church tomorrow, along with the prize marrows and potatoes and swedes.'

There was a hushed silence. Sarah flushed as red as the cherries in her hat and Guy and his sisters drew more closely round the pram.

'But of course Sarah will be only too glad,' said a voice, and looking up they saw that a tall young woman in a feathered hat now stood at the curate's side. 'I'm sure any Sunday School Scholar of mine will be proud to add her small mite to help beautify the church on such a happy occasion, won't you, my dear?'

'Then that's settled,' said the curate without listening to Sarah's muffled reply. And with a grateful smile, he whisked the corn doll from the pram and strode off with her tucked under his arm.

7   Let bygones be bygones

'She wasn't just your small mite to lend to the church but our corn doll as well,' said Rose as they hurried up the church path, after looking in vain for the corn doll through the windows of the curate's lodgings. 'Now if we can't find her we'll never be able to wish ourselves back to our own time without her.'

'Of course we'll find her,' said Sarah. 'She's bound to be in the church. All the decorations must have been done by now. Probably Miss Swithin helped the curate herself. She and Mr Watson are engaged to be married.'

After the bright sunlight they were glad to lift the latch of the church door and step into the coolness of the vaulted building. No one was about and, as Sarah had expected, the decorations were completed.

Poppy was seated between two sheaves of corn on the chancel steps. A striped marrow stood at her back and well-polished apples bordered her feet. One tasselled arm rested on a pile of purple cabbages and the other on a pyramid of bronze-skinned onions. Encircling her all around were Michaelmas daisies, bright-petalled dahlias, and trails of rose-red Virginia creeper.

'Miss Swithin and Mr Watson must have taken ages to do all that,' said Sarah Tinkley. 'We can't move her yet.'

'Of course I must stay,' said Poppy. 'Miss Swithin said I was to be the centrepiece of the arrangement. She and the reverend gentleman did it together, adding first one vegetable and then another. With a tortoiseshell butterfly or two I'll not lack for company, and after so much gadding about this will be restful. When you've once been thrown out and named as a heathen idol this is just what is needed.'

The church glowed with colour. It was as if a whole box of jewels had been tossed into the great stone building, and the brightest colour of all was the golden straw of their corn doll.

'She ought to stay till after the service at least,' whispered Bell. 'She'll be dreadfully disappointed if we don't let her, and so will Miss Swithin and the curate after they've both taken so much trouble.'

'But we can't wait,' objected Guy. 'That service isn't till tomorrow.'

'If it's time that fusses you,' pointed out the corn doll, 'that stops while you're away. Going anywhere with me is the same as a dream. Hours and hours go by and it only takes the tick of a minute. None of you will be missed back at the farm. Sarah and I stayed two months on a desert island and that took only from cockcrow to milking.'

'All the same we would have to make arrangements,' said Guy. 'We should have to sleep somewhere and we can't risk using our old rooms at the farm.'

'But so long as you don't light matches you'll be safe in the hay-loft back at the farm,' Sarah told them. 'No one will be up there except the farm cats and a mouse or two.'

'This isn't really taking any time at all,' Guy reminded his sisters in the loft as they tossed and turned in the hay, but in spite of his words the hot summer night seemed long and by dawn they were all hungry.

'Sarah promised to bring us something to eat directly she went down to see to that stove,' Rose told the others. 'I gave her one of Guy's Victorian half-crowns to pay for butter and milk and she said there would be enough for plenty of bread. They bake it on the farm in the old bread oven.'

Sarah arrived at cockcrow before anyone stirred in the house. With her she had brought a pitcher of milk, a plate of bread and butter, and six hard-boiled eggs.

'There's threepence change from your half-crown,' she announced. 'As for the corn doll – I've the afternoon off. I'll fetch her from the church and meet you outside sharp at two when I'm through with the washing-up.'

They did not dare attend the Harvest Festival Service that morning. Instead, they sat in the shadow of a yew tree in the churchyard and listened as the congregation sang the familiar words of the opening hymn:

> *Come, ye thankful people, come,*
> *Raise the song of Harvest-home;*
> *All is safely gathered in,*
> *'Ere the winter storms begin.*

But without Sarah Tinkley they still felt scared. Hay clung to the girls' brushed-nylon nightdresses, and they felt unwashed and untidy. Already they were hungry again and worse still they were thirsty.

'Couldn't we use that pump in the yard while everyone's in church?' asked Bell. 'We've still got that broken cup Sarah brought with the milk.'

But Guy refused to let them.

'The people at the farm would be used to drinking that well-water,' he said, 'but it might easily upset us. Mr Dawkings stopped using that well except for the stock ages ago.'

'Then let's look for a cottage that sells ginger-beer,' suggested Rose. 'I'm sure I noticed one in the village yesterday, and we've still got Sarah's threepenny-bit change and two of your Victorian shillings.'

They found the thatched cottage that sold picture postcards and minerals at the far end of the village. A sign announced that Cyclists and Tourists were catered for. A cobbled path led up to a rustic porch covered with roses and honeysuckle and the door was ajar.

A very old man appeared in answer to their timid knock. He peered at them through the misted lenses of a pair of almond-shaped gold-rimmed spectacles as he brought them stone bottles of ginger-beer and set them on a marble-topped table under the apple trees.

'There's gingerbread,' he told them when Rose asked if they might have something to eat, 'or Garibaldi biscuits, best sweet tea, Bath buns or Genoa pound cake.'

They chose best sweet tea biscuits and apples which he brought on a plate decorated with grapes and pears.

As they ate the old man stood near by with the sun shining on his watch-chain, his starched collar with rounded ends, and his grey knitted jacket.

'You've come from far?' he asked. 'I don't recollect seeing you in these parts afore.'

'London,' said Rose, 'but we're staying quite near.'

'In lodgings,' said Bell.

'Oh aye – you'll be on holiday then,' said the old man.

The sun was hot and there seemed a good deal of time to spare. Bees buzzed round the straw hives under the apple trees. The last of the ginger-beer poured from the stone bottles tasted better than any fizzy drinks they had ever sampled. Afterwards, as they munched the apples the old man told them about his life as a soldier in the Crimean war. He showed them the medal he had won and a tin of chocolate which Queen Victoria herself had sent him when in battle.

After their rest they made their way towards the church. The congregation had dispersed and most of the inhabitants of the village were at lunch. From the open windows drifted scents of roast beef and Yorkshire pudding and hot apple pie.

'We'd better stay near the church now till Sarah comes,' Guy told them, and hidden in the long grass and dog daisies behind the churchyard wall they fell asleep.

When Sarah aroused them an hour later they knew at once that something was wrong.

'It's her,' said Sarah. 'She's been took!'

Her cheeks were streaked with tears. Under her cloak her apron was stained with gravy from the washing-up. Black stockings wrinkled round her ankles and her heavy boots were white with dust.

'I came out without changing to save time,' she said, 'but it was still too late. Everything in the church had needed to be cleared early because of a wedding to-morrow. The Squire and his lady came with a dog cart from the big house. They've taken her away with the fruit and vegetables and the loaf like a sheaf of corn.'

'But where to?' asked Guy as Sarah sat down and mopped her nose with a red-spotted handkerchief.

'The children in the workhouse at Stonegate,' said Sarah. 'That's five miles from here along the main road.'

'Then we'll have to fetch her back,' said Rose. 'The Squire and his wife can't really have thought that the workhouse children would want her.'

'It wasn't for the children that they took her,' said Sarah. 'The lady, who is in the church now arranging maidenhair fern and carnations for the wedding, told me that the Squire meant to give her specially to the Work-house Master who's interested in folk-lore and old things to do with the countryside – bygones was what the Squire called them. He said our corn doll was a remarkably fine example and that he knew the Workhouse Master would be delighted to have her.'

The road to Stonegate stretched before them dusty and empty in the heat of the afternoon. None of them knew what they would be able to do when they reached the workhouse. They only knew they had to be there. With them they pushed the pram still filled with the summer flowers which Rose had tried to keep fresh in jam jars filled with water from the tap in the churchyard.

'If only we can find the corn doll we'll leave the pram behind as a toy for the orphans,' said Guy. 'We can always make Poppy another.'

They were very tired when at last they came to the outskirts of the market town. The cottage gardens were bright with flowers, but as they trailed up the main street they caught sight of alleyways where pale children with bare feet played round the doorways of tumbledown tenements.

As Sarah urged them onwards, for a second they paused to stare at the tightly-packed goods in a grocer's shop window. Even the names on the labels were strange and part of a country and Empire they had never known.

'Best Trinidad cocoa,' repeated Rose, 'citron candied peel, beef jelly, Bengal Club chutney, Rangoon rice, Chyloong ginger, household jam, gravy soup.'

'Darjeeling tea,' said Guy, 'knife polish, and blanc-mange.'

'And whatever are cowslip wax candles?' Bell asked. 'Or Russian isinglass and Best London Mottled soap?'

But Sarah Tinkley only hustled them on past a mantle-makers, and a sweet shop, and a toy shop full of wax-faced dolls and red-coated lead soldiers.

The workhouse was made of great blocks of Portland stone. Spiked railings guarded it from the road. Even the flower-beds were planted in patterns and edged with whitewashed stones.

'It's like a castle,' said Rose as they peered through the railings.

'Or a prison,' said Bell with a shiver.

Beside them Sarah didn't hesitate. She walked straight through the gate beside the porter's lodge into a gravelled quadrangle, and the others followed her.

Every stone in the yard was tidy and swept into place. Not a weed sprouted beside the flagstaff or the notices to keep off the grass. Only the four of them were bedraggled and out of place. With their eyes screwed up against the sun they stared across the yard. Nothing moved. Only a single golden straw lay tangled in the blossoms of a red geranium planted in the flowerbed before the Workhouse Master's house.

'That's from her,' whispered Sarah. 'Unless you carry her careful bits come loose, though I re-stitched her last Michaelmas with cobbler's thread.'

As she spoke the door of the lodge opened behind them.

'It's the porter,' said Rose; 'he's seen us and he's coming this way!'

For a second they stood rooted to the spot, then Sarah pushed them before her through a doorway at the side of the building. As they stood beside her in a flagged passage hardly daring to breathe, from the distance came the sound of children's voices like the chattering of sparrows.

'Come on,' said Sarah. 'We daren't stay here.'

She hurried them down the corridor and pushed open a pair of swing doors. Before them was a long vaulted hall. The sun shone through high lancet windows on to the bent heads of pinafored children seated at long deal tables set with the loaf shaped like a sheaf of wheat, the golden rolls of farmhouse butter, the honeycombs, fresh eggs, fruit and pots of plum jam which had been in the church. The children were too intent on their meal to notice Sarah and the others in the doorway, and a plump woman in *pince-nez* spectacles busy behind the tea urn at the central table never raised her head.

'Quick!' said Sarah. 'Push the pram under the table then put on these and sit down.'

From a near-by peg she grabbed four holland pinafores. Robed in these and with the pram hidden by the tablecloth, they wriggled on to a bench set in front of one of the side tables, just as the door behind them swung open and the porter glanced in.

'Anyone here, Miss, who didn't ought to be?' he asked the mistress in charge. 'I thought I saw four nippers slip in through the main gates and make off across the yard.'

'They've not come in here, Porter, I assure you,' the mistress said, glancing down the crowded tables while Guy and the others hid their faces behind upraised mugs of tea. 'Everything's quite in order.'

As the porter hurried off, at Sarah's side an older girl with straight red hair giggled.

'You've a cheek, Sarah Tinkley, and no mistake coming here with your friends and sitting down bold as brass for the Harvest Festival tea. After ten years of the workhouse I'd have thought you would have had enough and not chosen to come back even today.'

Sarah flushed. Rose and the others drew closer to her side. Suddenly they understood why she knew her way about the workhouse so well and the reason she had been sent out to service while still so young.

'It's not the tea we're after,' Sarah whispered, 'but the corn doll that was brought from the church by mistake along with the fruit and flowers. The Master will have her in his house by now with all his curiosities and by-gones.'

The red-headed orphan stared with a slice of bread and strawberry jam raised to her lips.

'You never mean to take her back?' she asked. 'That's picking and stealing like in the catechism.'

'She's ours and we've the right,' insisted Sarah. 'Picking and stealing have no part in it or I would have had none of it, and that you should know very well, Maisie Parker.'

'She really does belong to us,' whispered Rose, 'and it's not as if she was a proper doll that any of the children here would want. She's just important to us. In the winter time she's all the company Sarah has, especially at night.'

'And we're going to leave a doll's pram behind,' said Bell. 'It's under the table.'

Maisie Parker lifted the tablecloth to peer underneath. The pram's blue and yellow paint shone bright in the dim light.

'It's only hand-made,' said Guy, 'but we'd like them to have it.'

'I dare say there's one or two who would fancy it,' said Maisie. 'At least it's brand-new and not secondhand. But how do you mean to take back that doll?'

'We shan't be able to do it unless you can help,' said Sarah. 'We'll have to be in and out of the Master's room quick as lightning. The best way will be to slip in when his tea-table is cleared.'

'That's my job as Senior Girl,' said Maisie, 'though I take one or two of the juniors if there's much to carry.'

'That's what I thought,' said Sarah. 'All we want is for you to let us do it instead.'

The Workhouse Master's house was reached through a red baize door leading off the corridor. Once she had made her decision Maisie had been helpful. She had provided them with tea-trays and a crumb-scoop, and she had turned fiercely on two of the orphans who had gathered round after their meal to stare at Sarah and her companions.

'Never mind who they are. It's no concern of yours,' she had told them. 'Come along with me to look under the table and perhaps we'll find a surprise!'

'Maisie was no more than a little lass when I was in the workhouse,' Sarah told them as they made their way through the baize door. 'I did what I could for her and I guessed she wouldn't have forgotten. Next year she'll be set to work along of me up at Knack Gold.'

The Master's house smelt of beeswax polish and moth-balls. Cases of flint implements and Roman pottery lined the passage walls.

'It's like a museum,' whispered Rose. 'No wonder the Squire thought he'd be interested in the corn doll.'

Outside the sitting-room they halted. From the other side of the door came the sound of voices and the tinkle of tea-cups.

'He must be having a party,' whispered Rose. 'It seems awful to interrupt.'

Sarah took no notice but pressed her eye to the keyhole.

'She's in there all right between the pampas grass and a witch-doctor's mask, on top of the piano near the french windows. Now all we have to do is to go in and fetch her out – never mind how.'

'Won't the Workhouse Master recognize you?' asked Guy as Sarah tapped on the door.

'He's new since I left,' said Sarah and in answer to the Master's request, with the others beside her, she entered the room.

'If you please, Sir, I've come to clear away,' she told the small sandy-haired man who they guessed must be the Workhouse Master, 'and the others are here to help carry.'

Even as she and Guy loaded the first tea tray, while Bell and Rose edged across the crowded room towards the piano, footsteps sounded in the passage.

'It's that porter again,' whispered Bell. 'That's the way his boots squeak!'

As the porter stood panting in the doorway with his eyes fixed upon them, Bell dived for the corn doll and Guy pushed Sarah through the open French window.

'Run,' he whispered. 'They mustn't catch you. We'll be all right now we've got her!'

Sarah hesitated for an instant with the sun on her face.

'Don't forget those pinafores,' she said. 'You would never be able to explain them back at the farm and they'll have to be accounted for.'

Then, with her skirts gathered in her hand and her boots striking sparks from the gravel, she darted off across the garden.

'I'm sorry to intrude,' said the porter, 'but those are the children I saw making off across the yard not half an hour ago. They came in by the main gate without so much as a by your leave. I've been after them ever since – though there was another I could swear. A girl who knew her way about and was once in the children's ward of this workhouse or I'm a Dutchman!'

'Then go after her and be smart about it,' said the Master. 'There she is going over the garden wall!'

As the porter raced towards her Sarah Tinkley dropped down on the far side of the wall and made for the open country. For a while the porter panted after her, but soon she was no more than a dark speck moving across the harvest fields. Then she was lost in the distance and only the corn swayed over her.

In the sitting-room the Master of the Workhouse and his guests stared at Guy and his sisters. As Sarah had directed they had discarded their pinafores and they stood before the company in their crumpled clothes.

'Poor little waifs, they've hardly a stitch to their backs,' whispered one of the ladies in a dress with a bustle and train. 'I daresay they were only after a square meal.'

In the crowded room it was as if all the pictures of their great-great-aunts and uncles in the family photograph album had come to life and were looking down upon them with curiosity or disapproval.

'Now suppose you tell me what you are after?' said the Master.

'We're sorry to upset your tea party, sir,' said Guy. 'It's only the corn doll we came after.'

'She was brought with the fruit and the flowers from the church by mistake,' added Rose. 'The Squire took her without knowing she had only been lent.'

'And she really is ours,' said Bell as she clutched the doll in her arms. 'We could never part with her even if it meant going through fire and water to get her back.'

The Master sat down on the piano stool and mopped his brow.

'It's difficult to explain,' said Rose; 'that's why we thought it wasn't much use to try, but perhaps if you know about folk-lore you'll understand. You see, the corn doll isn't just an ordinary doll. She has magic power. Whoever finds her and really needs it she helps. That's why that other girl was with us. The corn doll belongs to her too. Ever since she left the workhouse to go into service on a lonely farm the doll's been her only friend.'

'Only that's in your time not ours,' said Guy. 'My

sisters and I really live years and years ahead. The corn doll just wished us back into the past because we wanted to warm up.'

'You see it's the spirit of the corn harvest she has,' explained Rose. 'It gives her the power to wish us backwards and forwards in time.'

'Like this,' said Bell, shaking several grains of wheat from the corn doll's husks into the others' hands. 'Each of us holds one of these grains – then we simply wish.'

'To be back where we belong,' said Rose with the grain of wheat pinched between her fingers.

As she spoke, and the Workhouse Master and his guests watched, the piano and the pampas grass and the witch doctor's mask grew dim as if mist swirled about the room. The sun shining on the geraniums in the flowerbeds faded, and Rose and Guy and Bell were in the attic once more with the wind rattling the slates on the roof and the newspapers shifting on the floor.

8 The tea party

'And that was what I call a trip,' said the corn doll when they rejoined her in the attic ten minutes later, dressed once more in their warmest clothes. 'There was something for everyone and a good regular eighty degrees. Summers were summers then and no mistake. The only pity was that none of you could be at that service. They had all the best hymns and not a pew was empty. When people are so appreciative I must say that it makes all my trouble with the harvest worth while.'

Poppy settled herself comfortably in her old corner by the mangle with her mouth shining and all the heads of corn nodding on her brow. Rose looked at the others and giggled.

'It isn't only your trouble,' Guy pointed out. 'If the farmer didn't put in good seed and roll and harrow it properly there wouldn't be much of a harvest anyway.'

'And it's God who arranges "the soft refreshing rain",' said Bell.

'Naturally we all pull together,' said the corn doll. 'I'd be the last to deny that. It's just that for once it was pleasant to have been of some account again. None of you has lived in the old times or seen one of the Harvest Home suppers with me right on the centre table all decked round with flowers and every man on the farm with his tankard raised to toast my health.'

'Then let's have a party now especially for you,' suggested Bell. 'After you've taken us out so often it would be only right.'

'And while we're getting it ready Guy will have time to make another pram,' said Rose. 'There's another apple box he can use, but he'll need to buy the wheels in Stonegate when Mr Dawkings drives in to the market.'

Their preparations for the party took several days. Out of doors the snow had melted. Only drifts still outlined the windward hedges and blackened heaps of snow edged the lanes where the snow-plough had forced a passage. In the yard the robin sang in the bare branches of the buddleia by the cattle trough. In the kitchen garden Mrs Dawkings put a barrel and two tea-chests over the rhubarb so that the first stems would grow long and pink in the dark. In the attic trays of seed potatoes were set to sprout, and Mr Dawkings was in and out of the farm at all hours caring for his ewes and the first lambs.

Mrs Dawkings was busy splitting up the largest of her maidenhair ferns when Rose asked her if they might hold the party up in the attic.

'Really it will be a dolls' tea party,' she explained, 'especially for the corn doll and we shouldn't need a fire.'

Mrs Dawkings plunged her kitchen knife into the fern and with two cuts divided it into four. When the last plant was bedded in its new pot she looked up with the fern leaves curved about her face.

'There's no reason not to have a party so long as you've a mind to it,' she said. 'This weather likely it will put heart into 'ee.'

The corn doll took a keen interest in all their preparations.

'Mostly at a Harvest Home Supper they had roast beef with a side of bacon and plum pudding to follow,' she told Bell and her sister. 'Then there were cakes and cut-rounds spread with jam and cream, and ale and cider that had been brewed on the farm.'

'She doesn't understand that food's different nowadays,' complained Rose. 'The sort she talks about is more like the food they ate in *Lorna Doone*, except for those cut-rounds which are just plain buns cut in half. But nowadays even Mrs Dawkings just buys fish-fingers and frozen peas from the deep freeze in the village shop.'

Eventually they found a very small Christmas pudding in the shop marked down to half-price, and some chicken and ham paste for sandwiches. Rose and Bell made cakes from puffed rice and melted chocolate, and they bought a box of iced fancy cakes from the baker who called at the farm. Instead of tea they had a bottle of raspberryade.

'We ought to have proper dolls' cups and saucers,' insisted Bell but finding any was a puzzle. Guy reported that even in Stonegate there was nothing to be found except cheap plastic. In the end Mrs Dawkings herself solved the problem. From a box in the kitchen dresser she took a doll's china tea-pot decorated with pink rosebuds, a cream jug with a faded gold rim, and four cups decorated with violets.

'If it's china you're short of these might come in handy,' she told Rose. 'I've kept them by from when Liza was a little lass.'

The party started at three in the afternoon while there was plenty of light.

'Strictly speaking there should be music,' Poppy pointed out, 'a fiddle or two at least and an accordion or a flute.'

'Then we'll have a comb band,' said Guy, 'with our hair combs and tissue paper.'

The band was a success. They played 'God Save the Queen' and 'Rule Britannia', the 'Marseillaise' and songs which Poppy had learnt from Sarah Tinkley: 'A Bicycle Made for Two' and 'Oh, Mr Porter'.

Soon it was dusk. Outside the sun sank like a red coal in the cold sky. The washing Mrs Dawkings carried in from the line was frozen stiff as cardboard. Inside the attic Guy lit a storm-lantern which Mr Dawkings had lent them. The light glowed on their faces and on Poppy's eyes as she sat in the new pram which Guy had just completed. It was filled with flowers they had made from crêpe paper.

'When you're gone it will be mortal quiet,' said the corn doll as Bell reached over to eat up the chocolate cake on her plate. 'No doubt your parents will want you home soon.'

'They're out of hospital now and they've found another flat,' Rose told her. 'We can go home some time next week directly they've fixed up about the furniture.'

'Then you'll have new dolls of your own,' said Poppy with her eyes on Bell. 'A birthday and a Christmas or two and the numbers will soon be made up.'

In the shadowed attic no one spoke. A sparrow rustled under the eaves as it settled down for the night. The corn doll's shadow was crooked on the wall with her arms outstretched and the ears of corn tumbled on her head.

Bell's head was bent and she did not look at the corn doll when she spoke.

'None of the new dolls people will give us could ever be as good as you.'

'And we've all wondered,' said Rose, 'and Guy thought it wouldn't hurt to ask because you can always say "no", but we've all wondered if when we do go home ...'

'You would come with us?' said Bell. 'We know it wouldn't be like the real country but there will be Kensington Gardens, and mother says the new flat has a balcony over the front porch where we can have window-boxes and plants.'

'And there would be a proper cradle,' said Rose, 'and a

real doll's pram, not just one we've made ourselves. Bell's big doll's pram was burnt in the fire and the insurance people have replaced it already.'

'Rose and Bell would like it more than anything,' added Guy, 'and so should I.'

Poppy bent forward as Bell mopped a spot of raspberryade from her spotted skirt. One of the ears of corn brushed her hand.

'There's nothing I'd fancy more than to go with you,' she said, 'but it wouldn't do. My place is here on the farm especially now when things don't look too bright. That was what I was made for. Nowadays, with weedkiller and chemicals, it might seem that there's no place for me, but that's as may be. My duty is here should the time come and I'm ever needed, and that's where I must stop.'

No one argued. They had half-expected her answer before it was given. The corn doll was a part of Knack Gold Farm, and if times were bad they knew that no power or discomfort would ever make her desert it.

'Then we'll come and see you just as often as we can,' said Bell.

'And I'll always be here ready to welcome you,' said the corn doll, 'so long as my straws hold together and there's corn in my husks.'

9 The day after tomorrow

A south-west gale shook the farmhouse the next morning. Doors slammed and buckets clattered across the yard. The cockerel's bronzed tail-feathers bent in the wind as he escorted his hens into the shelter of the outbuilding below the hay loft. Polythene feed bags wrapped themselves round the gate posts and floated half-submerged in the water trough. Poppy was slumped in her pram in the corner of the attic fast asleep, and everyone on the farm seemed in a bad temper.

Clearing up the remains of the doll's tea party after breakfast no one fancied the last of the iced cakes.

'The icing hurts my tooth,' said Guy. 'Directly we're home again I'll have to go to the dentist.'

Already as they neared the end of their stay they felt restless, as if they were sitting in a railway train waiting for it to pull off from the platform.

Downstairs the house felt colder than usual. Mrs Dawkings was busy with the washing. Long coils of sheets lay coiled like sea serpents in the yellow plastic basket ready to be hung on the line, and small whites boiled on the stove. She looked tired and worried as she stood at the sink. Propped behind the china dogs on the mantelshelf they saw several buff envelopes which they guessed must be bills.

'We haven't been anywhere with Poppy for ages,' complained Bell as they stared at copies of *The Farmer and Stockbreeder* in the front parlour. 'Once we're home we'll always be sorry we didn't ask her to take us to lots more places.'

Rose shivered. One of the bills they had noticed in the kitchen had been for electricity, and neither of them had liked to switch on the electric fire.

'All right, we'll ask Guy and see what he thinks.'

'You and Rose can go anywhere you like,' Guy told them when they found him in the outhouse making a pair of book-ends to take home to their mother. 'I'm staying here. Going backwards you may land up anywhere doing anything. So long as it was summer Poppy just wouldn't care. It's like reversing downhill with your eyes shut.'

'But nothing really awful has happened to us so far,' argued Bell, 'and all the people have been friendly. Not even that Workhouse Master was horrid but only surprised.'

'And if we'd never been anywhere we shouldn't have met Tansy and Kate or Sarah Tinkley,' pointed out Rose.

Guy was silent as he finished painting the second book-end. Now that the first coat was on they knew that he would have to leave the book-ends to dry.

'Apart from everything else,' he said as he put the paint brush into a jar of turpentine substitute, 'in the past, even just a few years ago, there's always this bother with clothes. In the last war if you hadn't been wearing trousers your skirts would have been miles too short. Those Victorian nightdresses helped last time but they still looked peculiar and I felt like a tramp in jeans.'

'Then if you won't go backwards,' said Rose, 'why don't we ask to go forward just a little way? That couldn't hurt, and if it was warm we could bathe in that sandy part of the river just by the bridge.'

'We'll say some time this next summer,' said Bell. 'Then Poppy can't possibly make a mistake.'

Poppy was sitting upright in her pram when they re-entered the attic. The frilled paper cup from one of the shop cakes was stuck to her skirt but she looked wide awake.

'Of course it's possible,' she told them when they suggested the trip. 'Only going forward can be tricky. Even next summer is not what I would choose.'

'But it's so much easier,' said Rose, 'and Guy won't come at all if we do anything else.'

'Very well,' said the corn doll, 'only this time you'll have to wish carefully. Make one slip and we'll end up well past 2000 A.D. That's not to my fancy even if it's yours.'

With the grains of wheat in their cold fingers they wished. It was like pushing off from the side of a swimming pool in a smooth dive. Closing their eyes they almost felt the rush of water over their heads and the cool green darkness pressing against their eyelids.

As the sun blazed through the window they blinked. The yard below was full of people. Cars, Land-Rovers, and cattle trucks were parked all down the farm track. Around them in the attic lay bundles of stair rods, rolls of tattered matting, and zinc baths full of oddments. On each lot a numbered label was glued.

'It's an auction sale,' whispered Guy. 'Look out there – the sheep and cows have been penned. Everything's being sold. There's the farm tractor, and the disc harrow, and the hay turner, and all the old wooden hay-making rakes. The Dawkings must be selling up and leaving the farm.'

'That's what Mrs Dawkings always dreaded might happen,' said Rose. 'Don't you remember how worried she was about all that rain?'

As she spoke, footsteps sounded in the outer attic and a couple with sale catalogues in their hands pushed open the door.

'Most of this will be just junk,' said the man. 'There's no sense in rummaging round – especially in this heat.'

'No harm in just looking,' said the woman. 'These youngsters seem to have found something already. What's the number of that quaint old corn doll in the pram?' she asked Bell.

'Poppy hasn't a number and she's not for sale,' said Bell, snatching up the doll. 'She belongs to us.'

With Poppy clutched in Bell's arms they made for the door and clattered down the stairs.

In Guy's bedroom they saw the roach and the sparrow-hawk in a sale lot with the farm magazines. Outside on the broad landing window-sill stood Lot 108: 'Sundry Potted Plants'.

'There are those maidenhair ferns Mrs Dawkings split up,' said Rose, 'and her best pelargoniums.'

'And all the ornaments from the parlour are on our old chest-of-drawers,' Bell reported as she squeezed her way through the crowd: 'those china spaniels and the view of Lynmouth done on a slice of wood, and the red tablecloth with the bobbled fringe.'

'Do come on,' urged Guy, 'or we'll meet Mrs Dawkings. She's bound to be about. I noticed Mr Dawkings over by the cow-shed talking to the auctioneer.'

'She'll mind so much about leaving the farm,' said Rose as they followed Guy downstairs. 'So will Mr Dawkings – she always said farming was his whole life.'

In Bell's arms Poppy's straw body shook.

'I warned the lot of you,' she whispered. 'Seeing round the next corner's not always agreeable.'

Dust hung in a gold haze over the farmyard. Set out in one of the open-fronted barns they saw all the farm implements arranged in lots. They saw the scythes, and sickles, and swaphooks with their handles polished by long hours of labour, the pitchforks, and oddments of harness. They saw the trug basket in which Mrs Dawkings had always collected the eggs, the spokeshave Guy had used when he had helped mend the farm gate, and several pots of paint.

'That's the pot of white I was using for the book-ends and it's not even gone hard,' said Guy, 'so this can't be longer away than next summer.'

Suddenly, as they left the outhouse for the farmyard, Guy tugged his sisters behind a trailer laden with the sections of a henhouse.

'There's Liza Dawkings,' he said, 'with her grandmother by that table with the tea-urn near the back door. She must be taking her summer holidays and have come down from London to help.'

'And she's coming this way,' said Rose. 'I'm sure she's seen us.'

'Then let's hide,' said Guy. He raced up the stone

steps which led to the hay-loft and his sisters darted after him.

Even so it was too late.

'You'd better come out! I know you're here,' said Liza as she stood in the sunlit doorway. 'I would have spotted those clothes that I helped you to choose anywhere.'

Scrambling from behind the bales of hay they stood before Liza. For a second no one spoke.

'You found her then,' said Liza with her eyes on the corn doll. 'I fancied you might when I sent the lot of you down here, and I said there'd be advantages but I never told you straight out in case she turned difficult. It's not everyone she takes to or is willing to look after.'

'Liza and I are old friends,' explained the corn doll. 'After her mother died she spent most of her time here.'

'I thought you must have meant us to find her,' said Rose, 'but she never said anything about you so I was never sure.'

'Having her with us has made all the difference, especially to Bell,' added Guy.

'We've been backwards twice,' said Bell, 'and this time we thought we'd go forward . . .'

'Only we never dreamt it would turn out like this,' said Guy, 'with everything being sold and Mr and Mrs Dawkings both leaving.'

Liza's face clouded as she sat down on a bale of hay. Her bright clothes seemed to have lost their shine like the plumage of an injured bird.

'It's not what Grandfather and Grandma would have chosen,' she told them. 'If they'd had their way the pair of them would have stayed on for years yet, but they've been forced to sell up and quit.'

'But what's happened?' asked Rose. 'Is it something to do with the wheat crop? Mrs Dawkings was worried that the damp weather might spoil it when we first came.'

'And she had cause to be,' said Liza. 'You'll see what all the rain this last winter and spring has done the moment you set foot in the cornfield. Ever since I came here to live when I was small things haven't been too good. Time and time again my grandfather has had to draw on his savings or go to the bank for help, and when this season's wheat crop failed he just had no money left.'

Liza brushed her hand across her eyes and sniffed as Mrs Dawkings called for her in the yard below.

'Now I'll have to go,' she said, 'and you'd be wise to make for the fields and not hang about here where you might be seen. It's hard when folk work all their lives only to see what they've made sold up to strangers, but that's a risk all farmers know they run and my grandfather and mother wouldn't want you to worry your heads over it.'

Liza paused for a second to straighten the corn doll's cape, then without another word she turned on her heel and ran down the steps.

As they watched her disappear in the crowd none of them spoke. They thought of Liza's kindness to them all on the night of the fire when their own home had been destroyed. Now it was Liza's home which the auctioneer was selling piece by piece. They were glad to do as she had suggested and to make for the cornfield out of earshot of the sound of the bidding.

As they followed the field path beside the hedge they saw that the wheat was fully grown. A breeze sang in the cornheads and the blades of corn moved like the ripples on a windswept lake.

'I don't see what Liza meant was wrong,' said Rose as she shaded her eyes from the sun. 'The corn looks just ready to harvest.'

In Bell's arms Poppy shifted impatiently.

'That's where you're wrong,' she said. 'There won't be a harvest fit to cut this year.'

'But why?' asked Guy.

'Look for yourselves,' said the corn doll. 'Look at the leaves and the stems and the cornheads.'

Kneeling on the stony path they stared along the furrows.

'Run your finger down one of the leaves,' ordered Poppy.

Guy did so, and when he lifted his finger the others saw that it was coated with ginger powder.

'Now look at that grain,' said the corn doll.

Rose took a head of the wheat between her fingers and shook the grains into the palm of her hand. In the sunlight she saw that instead of being plump and shining the grains were black and shrivelled.

'That's rust,' said Poppy quietly. 'Damp makes the spores grow. It spreads right through a field and into all the fields around. The best thing to do now is to scrap the crop and plough again.'

No one spoke. The sun was hot on their shoulders. High above a lark sang as it mounted towards the sun. Already cattle trucks and Land-Rovers loaded with furniture, rolls of wire netting, and pig troughs, made their way along the rough track which led from Knack Gold to the main road.

All their eyes were set on the corn doll. They saw her body bound with twine, the ears of corn on the top of her head, and her red-spotted shawl and yellow skirt which had been faded by so many summers. The sun glinted on her eyes, dazzling their own. When Guy spoke he spoke for them all.

'But if it's your job to look after the crops on the farm why did you let this happen?'

In the silence Bell and Rose looked away. Only the wind still moved through the corn. It was as if a cloud had blotted out the sun.

When the corn doll spoke her voice was strong.

'In farming there's always defeat as well as victory. That's got to be reckoned with. This time I've failed. That's fair enough but it's not the end. Remember, there's still a little time we have in hand. The future is not fixed like the past. Now we'll need to go back. After that it will be up to me.'

10 Straw in the wind

Standing once more in the attic after they had wished themselves back, they shivered. The attic felt colder than it had ever felt before. The gale had not lessened. It roared round the chimney-stacks and tore at the slates above their heads. Now and then a loose slate slithered off the roof of one of the barns and splintered on the cobbled yard below.

Poppy lay where they had put her in the pram, with all the crêpe flowers that they had made still about her. She stared up at the ceiling without uttering another word.

After all that had happened they felt hungry yet sick as well.

'I wish we'd never been into the future,' said Bell. 'Now we know what's going to happen here we shan't even enjoy being at home with Mummy and Daddy again in the new flat.'

'Poppy will stop the farm having to be sold – you'll see,' whispered Rose. 'She said that there was a little time in hand. What happens in the future doesn't have to happen like things have happened in the past. That's what she meant when she said the future wasn't fixed.'

But none of them could see what the corn doll would be able to do, and she herself gave no further explanation.

'But if so much is going wrong with the corn why doesn't Mr Dawkings plough it all up and put in fresh seed?' asked Bell. 'He's said again and again that he wished he'd waited to make a spring sowing.'

'And it's only the beginning of February now, so there would be plenty of time,' added Rose.

'Of course there would be,' said Guy, 'only he hasn't the money to start all over again and the Bank can't lend him any more. I heard him talking to Mrs Dawkings about it one day when we were waiting for you to come down to breakfast.'

Long after the others had gone downstairs Bell sat beside Poppy hunched in her anorak with the hood pulled up over her head.

'We didn't mean to sound angry or rude back there in the cornfield,' said Bell. 'It was just that we're so used to you being able to manage and we couldn't understand how everything had gone wrong.'

The corn doll scarcely stirred.

'No offence was taken where none was intended,' she said stiffly.

'Then won't you change your mind and come home with us when we go next week?' asked Bell. 'If the farm does have to be sold anything might happen if you stay here.'

The corn doll lifted her head and looked at Bell. The heads of corn tossed proudly in the wind, and her eyes were suddenly like coals of fire.

'If I can't save Knack Gold Farm I shan't be here,' she said, 'but what power I have will be used.'

Bell couldn't sleep that night. The wind shook the window and moaned in the chimney. She thought of

Poppy alone in the attic. Whatever the corn doll might have said about not taking offence, Bell knew that their words of reproach must have hurt her feelings.

As she lay wakeful in the moonlight, from the attic above she heard the window blowing on its hinges. Listening to the casement window banging to and fro Bell thought of the rain blowing in on the corn doll as she slept in her pram. On such a night her straw would be drenched. Without pausing to wake Rose, Bell reached for her torch, slipped on her dressing-gown and slippers, and crept from the room.

Rose woke as the central light of the room dazzled her eyes. Bell stood in the doorway with Guy at her side.

'It's the corn doll,' said Guy. 'Bell says she's gone!'

'The attic window was banging so I went up to latch it,' Bell explained, 'and when I looked to see if Poppy was all right her pram was empty.'

'She doesn't seem to be anywhere in either of the attics, but we wanted you to come and make sure,' said Guy. 'Bell's scared that she's done something desperate to help save the farm, and if she has it's because of what we said yesterday.'

As they stood together in the attic the beams from their torches lit up every cobwebbed corner. With Rose to help him Guy shifted the trunks and boxes in both the inner and the outer rooms, but of the corn doll they could find no trace.

'She's disappeared into thin air,' said Guy with a shiver.

As he spoke Bell called from the window of the inner attic.

'Look, there's a piece of straw lodged on the sill!'

Guy unlatched the window and together they peered out. Below in the moonlit farmyard they fancied they saw a shape like a tussock of straw blown hither and thither by the gale.

'I'm sure that's her!' cried Bell.

'Then we'll have to go after her,' said Guy. 'She could be blown to pieces on a night like this.'

They paused only to put on gum-boots with their trousers and duffle coats over their night clothes. Then they raced downstairs and drew back the bolts of the back door. The gale almost tugged the door from their grasp as they shut it behind them and edged their way across the yard.

The moon rode through ragged clouds high overhead. Straw and dead leaves beat in their faces. A piece of polythene from a rick cover whirled through the air and twisted like a black serpent round their legs.

'Keep tight hold of me and Guy,' Rose warned Bell. 'Don't try and stand up alone.'

There was no sign of Poppy in the yard.

'I believe she's making for the cornfield,' said Rose. 'That's where she would feel she ought to be.'

With their boots slipping and sliding in the mud they made their way towards the cornfield.

'That's her in the thorn tree by the gate,' shouted Guy. 'You can see her spotted cape tangled in the branches.'

They raced forward but the gale was faster. The ragged bundle of straw was tossed away into the darkness. Only the doll's cape was left spiked on the thorns.

'We must find her quickly,' sobbed Bell with the torn cape crumpled in her hand. 'Poppy won't care what

happens to herself so long as she saves the farm. She told me she'd use all the power she had to do that.'

They ran on into the cornfield. The waterlogged furrows sucked at their boots and the short blades of wheat bent before the wind like blown fur. The wind spun them round so that they lost all sense of direction. They only knew that they were somewhere in the centre of the ten-acre field and that the air around them was full of blowing pieces of straw. With hands still linked they stumbled forward. Once something struck Rose's face and she found a dry head of wheat lodged in the neck of her duffle coat.

In the darkness it seemed impossible that the corn doll hadn't already been torn to pieces. As they searched for any trace of her they thought of her other friends at the farm who had shared her company like themselves.

'If only Kate and Tansy, and Sarah Tinkley, and Liza were here they'd help,' said Bell. 'If only they knew the danger she was in they'd be bound to come.'

'Perhaps they do,' said Rose.

As she spoke, beside them in the darkness other figures raced. Kate in oiled sea-boot stockings and gum boots, Tansy in a khaki Balaclava hood, Sarah with her boots heavy with mud, and Liza in a gleaming white P.V.C. raincoat with a muddied scrap of yellow material grasped in her hand.

'It's her skirt torn to shreds,' she said as she faced them with her face white with anger. 'In a gale like this she'll be lost for ever. How could you let her do it?'

'It's the harvest she's trying to save,' shouted Guy. 'Nothing would have stopped her once she knew what was wrong.'

Afterwards, they only ran with no breath left in their bodies to speak. Once Bell fell flat on her face and the others tugged her to her feet. Then they ran on.

Suddenly in the darkness their faces were whipped with flying pellets that stung their cheeks.

'It's hail,' said Guy.

Beside him Rose halted and shone her torch on one of the pellets that lay in her hand.

'It's not hail,' she said as the others crowded round, 'it's a grain of wheat like one of the grains from the heads of wheat on the corn doll.'

No one spoke. Their eyes were fixed on a cloud of grain and broken straw that whirled about them with the corn shining in the darkness like chips from the sun itself.

As they stood silent Bell tugged her hand free and raced forward into the golden centre of the swirling grain.

As Rose and Guy ran towards her they knew that now except for Liza they were alone.

Bell knelt in the mud beside a tangle of twine and a few scraps of straw with the crescent and two five-pointed stars resting on the doll's cape in her hand.

'Poppy said she'd use all her power to save the crop,' Bell whispered; 'that's what she's done. Now it will be safe.'

Beside them Liza's face was angry no longer as she put her arm round Bell's shoulders.

'And so will the corn doll be too,' she told her as she took the doll's cape with the crescent and the two stars from Bell's cold fingers and wrapped them in the yellow cotton bound round with the tangled twine.

Then she was gone and they were alone. Together they trudged back to the farm with the moon shining clear on the rows of springing wheat.

They woke late the next morning. The wind had dropped and for the first time since their visit had begun sunlight shone into their rooms. What had happened in the night seemed like a dream but their mud-stained boots lay in a jumble where they had stepped out of them by the back door, and their duffle coats were still damp and spattered with straw.

'We ought to begin to pack,' Rose suggested after breakfast. 'It's bound to take some time. There will be much more to take home than what we brought.'

Even packing and washing anything that needed to be washed didn't take all the morning. Just before lunch Rose and Guy missed Bell.

Running upstairs they found her in the attic standing beside the mangle with her head bent over three grains of wheat that lay in her hand.

'They're all that are left,' she said. 'One was in my duffle coat pocket and the other two were lodged in a spider's web near the place where she used to sit.'

Rose looked at Guy. They knew Bell had been crying. Last night Liza's words had comforted them all, but now as they stood with Bell in the deserted attic it was hard to know exactly what Liza had meant.

'One thing's certain,' said Rose. 'Liza wouldn't have said what she did about the corn doll being safe unless she really believed it. Even if we don't understand we'll have to trust her.'

'And Mr Dawkings was up in the cornfield this morning,' said Guy. 'He told me that the gale last night has dried up the land and done a power of good. He could see a change in the wheat already. He thinks it's got a hold now and that it should really begin to move.'

'That's what the corn doll would have wanted,' said Rose. 'It's what she was meant for.'

Bell sniffed.

'Of course it was, but that doesn't help – it's her I want with us now.'

In spite of the winter sunlight they shivered. Without the corn doll the attic seemed dusty and bare.

Looking at his sisters Guy knew he must do something to help, yet he didn't know what.

'Let's each take one of the grains that Bell found and make one more wish,' he said. 'If they're from the corn doll they might still work.'

'What shall we wish?' asked Rose as they took the grains in their hands.

'The same as we wished last time,' said Guy, 'to go forward into the future just as far as we went before.'

They wished aloud with the words echoing in the attic.

The winter sunlight changed to that of summer. In the attic apples were set in racks, bronzed onions were spread on sheets of newspaper, and bags full of lavender and herbs hung from the rafters. In the yard drawn up in one of the open barns stood their father's car piled high with luggage.

'There's Father carrying a new set of golf-clubs in through the back door,' whispered Rose, 'and Mother with one of our new suitcases. We must have just come for a holiday.'

As she spoke footsteps sounded on the attic stairs.

'I thought I'd find you here,' said Liza, 'and now

she's finished I wanted you to be the very first to see her. They cut the ten-acre field yesterday and Grandfather let me take the very last corn still standing.'

In Liza's arms with the late August sun shining down on her sat the corn doll. Her starred eyes shone and her crescent mouth smiled. Her red-spotted cape was draped round her shoulders, her yellow cotton skirt was mended and washed, and the heads of corn on her arms and head stood up stiff and straight, plump with new corn.

'You can play with her now,' said Liza, 'then she's to come down and sit at the head of the table for the Harvest Home supper. I'm off to help get it ready now.'

Alone in the attic they stared at the corn doll. Bell cradled her in her arms and ran her finger along the stalks of golden straw.

'It was time for a good shake-up,' said the corn doll. 'That dusty I were you wouldn't credit. Now that Liza has re-done me with the last of the crop I'm as good as new.'

'Is it really you?' asked Rose. 'Even though Liza promised that you would be safe, after what you did we were afraid that we might never see you again and that all your power was used up.'

The corn doll rustled.

'Of course it's me,' she said. 'As for the power, that's in the corn new every year. So long as there's a crop and someone takes the pains to fashion me I'm safe enough, and I shall go on as long as there's wheat at Knack Gold Farm.'